Other Books by Kiki Swinson

PLAYING DIRTY

NOTORIOUS

WIFEY

I'M STILL WIFEY

LIFE AFTER WIFEY

THE CANDY SHOP

A STICKY SITUATION

STILL WIFEY MATERIAL

STILL CANDY SHOPPING

WIFE EXTRAORDINAIRE

WIFE EXTRAORDINAIRE RETURNS

CHEAPER TO KEEP HER

CHEAPER TO KEEP HER 2

THE SCORE

CHEAPER TO KEEP HER 3

CHEAPER TO KEEP HER 4

THE MARK

CHEAPER TO KEEP HER 5

DEAD ON ARRIVAL

THE BLACK MARKET

THE SAFE HOUSE, BLACK MARKET 2

PROPERTY OF THE STATE, BLACK MARKET 3

THE DEADLINE

PUBLIC ENEMY # 1

PLAYING WITH FIRE

BURNING SEASON

WHERE THERE'S SMOKE

AMBER ALERT

KIKI SWINSON

www.kensingtonbooks.com

DAFINA BOOKS are published by

Kensington Publishing Corp.
900 Third Avenue
New York, NY 10022

All Kensington Titles, Imprints, and Distributed Lines are available at special quantity discounts for bulk purchases for sales promotions, premiums, fund-raising, and educational or institutional use. Special book excerpts or customized printings can also be created to fit specific needs. For details, write or phone the office of the Kensington special sales manager: Kensington Publishing Corp., 900 Third Avenue, New York, NY 10022, attn: Special Sales Department, Phone: 1-800-221-2647.

The DAFINA logo is a trademark of Kensington Publishing Corp.

ISBN: 978-1-4967-4686-3

Library of Congress Control Number: 2024940673

First Kensington Hardcover Edition: December 2024

ISBN: 978-1-4967-4688-7 (ebook)

10 9 8 7 6 5 4 3 2 1

Printed in the United States of America

PROLOGUE

"GET THE FUCK OFF OF ME! YOU PIECE OF SHIT!"

I barked at him—my anger was starting to well up like a volcano. I had spit at him until I saw a chunk of my DNA dangling from his face. He immediately wiped off the spit and examined it in his hand. It all seemed like everything was going in slow motion, because after he took his eyes off his hand, he looked at me and I could instantly see that his pupils were opening and closing rapidly. His previous calm face eased into a sinister frown. He raised a closed fist and lunged right at me. I saw it coming and I tried to duck, but it was too late.

"Aggh!" I shrieked.

My hands flew up instinctively to my head in an attempt to stop him, but the blow plowed through to me, smack-dab on the right side of my head. The impact took me out and I hit the floor hard. *Boom!* My insides felt like they had been knocked out of place and I was dazed.

"You fucking bitch!" I heard him say while I was trying to stop my head from spinning. "Spitting on me! Are you fucking crazy? After all that I've done for you. And that's how you repay me?" he grunted as he loomed over me.

"You took my kids from me," I mustered up the will to say as I fought through the pain in my head.

"Fuck your kids!" His voice boomed and then he lunged at me again. I braced myself because I knew exactly what was coming next. *Boom!*

"You fucking bitch!" he roared, and reached down and grabbed a fistful of my hair and wrapped it around his hand. He lifted my head off the floor and forced it back down with his brute strength. The back of my head crashed to the floor with so much force that I thought my brain was going to shoot through the front and burst out through my forehead. I now knew what people meant when they got hit and said they were literally seeing stars. My head hit with so much force, flashes of lights invaded my eyesight for at least thirty seconds. I was dazed and confused, and the pain was like nothing I'd ever felt before.

"Please stop! You're hurting me!" I cried out, trying to pry his fingers from my hair, but he wasn't relenting.

"Shut up, bitch! You're gonna take this ass kicking tonight," he growled while digging his fingers deep into my scalp, clutching my hair at the roots and filling his palm up with it.

Then he began dragging me across the floor. Suddenly an excruciating pain shot through my scalp and radiated over my entire head. I swear, I had never felt pain like that in my head. It felt like my entire scalp was being ripped off. I started kicking and screaming.

"Please let me go. Let my fucking hair go!" I yelled and screamed, and then I kicked at him again.

This time my foot landed near his groin area. He flinched for a second, but the pain didn't last long at all, and he was back on me. This time he lunged at me with his face. My face was scrunched up and my eyes rolled into the back of my head. The impact felt like he had rattled every organ in my body. Sweat immediately began pouring out from every pore of my body. I gagged, but nothing came up from my stomach. My heart pounded painfully against my weakened chest bone and my stomach literally churned. I was wishing for death, because even that had to be better than what I was feeling at that moment.

"Leave my mommy alone," I heard a voice shout from the other side of the room. Instantaneously we both looked in that direction and saw my son pointing a gun directly at us. At that very moment I realized that the gun I was carrying in my waist had fallen out onto the floor. And now my son had it in his hand. My attacker didn't know this, but my son knew how to use and fire a gun properly. I had been teaching him how to hold and fire a gun since he was six years old. And right now, it looked like my son was going to be my savior.

"Hey, you better stop waving that gun around before you hurt somebody," he warned him as he stood straight up and started walking toward him.

"Leave my son alone," I shouted as I began to pull myself up off the floor.

"Your son better put that gun away before I take it from him," he warned me as he continued to walk toward Little Kevin.

I couldn't get up fast enough to get to this man before he grabbed ahold of Little Kevin. The adrenaline pumping inside of me became overwhelming as I scrambled in the direction of the man and my son. My only thoughts were to get to my son before he did, but it seemed like I was moving in slow motion. Before I knew it, I saw my attacker towering over my son as he stood there nervously with the gun pointed directly at him. Without a moment's notice he lunged toward my son and then I heard the gun go off twice.

Pop! Pop!

CHAPTER 1

Ava

"TIME TO GET UP," I SHOUTED FROM THE HALLWAY OUTSIDE OF my bedroom. It was six-thirty, April 10, 2024, on a Wednesday morning, time for the kids to get up and get ready for school. Normally, my husband, Kevin, would do this part, but he was out of town on business, so I had been stuck dragging the kids out of bed these past couple of days. Getting resistance was something of the norm with my little kiddos. They always procrastinated getting out of bed in the morning to go to school, so I prepped myself for the pushback.

I entered Little Kevin's room first because he was the hardest one to get out of bed. To my surprise he was already up. I figured he was downstairs, probably eating a bowl of cereal or something, so I went into Kammy's bedroom next. "It's time to get up, my darling," I said as I entered my baby girl's room. But just like Little Kevin, she wasn't in bed, either. I knew then that she had gone downstairs with her brother to eat breakfast, so I made my way down to the kitchen to see what my little kiddos were doing.

On my way I pictured cereal crumbs and spilled milk on the kitchen table, with the milk carton sitting a few inches away from the bowl at room temperature. I was sure Little Kevin and Kammy were fighting over who got to look at the pictures on the cereal box. When I turned the corner and made my way into the kitchen, I saw that it was empty. In seeing that Little Kevin and Kammy were nowhere in sight, I paused for a second and tried to collect my thoughts.

"Wait a minute," I mumbled to myself. Then I turned in the opposite direction and called out their names. "Kammy! Little Kevin, where are y'all?" I yelled out loud enough so that they could hear me throughout the entire house. But I got no answer. So I called their names again. "Kammy! Little Kevin, where are you?" I shouted even louder.

Paulina heard me calling the kids' names and appeared from her bedroom. She stood over the balcony of the hallway, dressed in her pajamas and robe. She looked down at me in the living-room quarters of the house.

"Are the kids in the room with you?" I asked her.

"No, they're not," she replied. "Have you checked the garage or outside?"

"I am now. But I want you to check the bathroom, all the closets, and underneath their beds, because it sounds like they're playing a game of hide-and-seek," I told her.

"They better not be . . ." Paulina's voice trailed off.

While Paulina searched upstairs, I started looking everywhere I could think of that the kids could hide. First I went into the garage and then I exited the house through the side door. When I realized they weren't out there, I walked back into the house and searched all the closets, underneath all the tables— still, there was no sign of them. This immediately became a cause for alarm and I panicked.

"Paulina, did you find them yet?" I shouted from the living room.

Paulina appeared on the balcony. "No," she responded somberly.

"Oh, my God, Paulina, where are my kids?" I asked helplessly. I was actually at a loss for words, and I couldn't think straight, either.

"I don't know, but they're not in the house, so they must be outside. Maybe the backyard," Paulina suggested as she made her way downstairs. I didn't wait for her. I raced back through the kitchen and headed toward the side door, which led to my backyard. I heard Paulina in the distance, so I knew that she was behind me, but I kept going. Finding out where my kids were was eating me up inside. By the time I made it around the corner of my house, I heard Paulina scream. It startled the hell out of me, and I stopped in my tracks. When I turned around and saw that she wasn't behind me, I realized the scream came from the house, so I ran back in that direction.

When I reentered my home, I saw Paulina standing in the kitchen, holding a note in her hand. I ran toward her and snatched it out of her hands. The first words I read were written in bold: DO NOT CALL THE COPS OR YOUR KIDS WILL DIE! Reading those words, I instantly became sick and wanted to vomit. Instead, I continued to read on: *Your kids are safe and will be returned to you if you pay their two-million-dollar ransom. You have seventy-two hours to come up with the money. If you don't, then you will never see your children again. And let me please remind you that you must not call the cops. If you do, your kids will die! On the third day, phone us at 555-694-1138 and we will be in touch with ransom delivery instructions.*

"Oh, my God, Paulina, these people have my kids!" I screamed and broke down into tears. Paulina embraced me and held me tight. She tried to calm me by saying, "Don't worry! We're gonna get them back."

"But what if we don't, Paulina? They're asking for two million dollars." I became doubtful.

"We gotta think positive. Now, let's get Mr. Frost on the phone and he will come home, get the money together, and we can have our babies home by tonight," she assured me while handing me the cordless phone, which was nearby on the island.

I dialed my husband's cell phone number, and it rang five times before he answered.

"Hello," he said, sounding as if he had just woken up.

"Kevin," I screamed through the phone. Fear had penetrated my entire heart and placed a dark cloud over my head. It felt like I was drowning in heartache and confusion. I couldn't quite put my thoughts together, either. It felt like I was losing all my senses.

"What's wrong?" he replied.

"The kids are gone. Someone took them," I added.

"What do you mean, 'Someone took them'?" My outburst definitely alarmed him.

"Someone kidnapped them, Kevin." I began to cry.

"How do you know that?"

"Because they're not here and I'm holding a ransom note in my hand."

"What fucking ransom note?" His voice screeched. "What does it say?"

"It says that we have your kids, and if you want them back, you must come up with two million dollars. Right now, they are fine. But if you call the cops, you will never see them again. Someone will get in touch with you very soon with drop-off instructions," I paraphrased.

He shouted through the phone. "Is that it?"

"Yes, that's all that's in this letter."

"When did you find it?"

"After I searched the entire house for the kids."

"Where did you find the letter?"

"On the kitchen table."

"How long ago did you find the letter?"

"A few minutes ago."

"Wait, what time is it?" he asked. I could hear him shuffling things around in the background.

"It's a little after seven o'clock," I managed to say.

"Where is Paulina?"

"She's right here, standing next to me."

"Did she stay there last night?"

"Yes."

"Did she hear anything?"

"She said she didn't."

"What time did you guys go to bed last night?"

"The kids were in bed around ten o'clock. Paulina, a little bit after that. I probably dozed off around midnight." I continued to cry. Tears saturated my face.

"So that means they were taken sometime after midnight and just before dawn?" Kevin calculated aloud.

This announcement hurt me to the core, and I screamed out in agony. "Noooooo! Don't say that," I cried out once more. The pain was becoming unbearable.

"Ava, this is not the time to break down. We've got to stay strong and positive," Kevin coached me.

"I know, Kevin, but those are my babies, and we need to hurry up and get them back," I whined, and with good reason.

"And we will," Kevin said. Then he fell silent for a couple of seconds. My sobs were all you could hear.

"This just doesn't make any sense. I mean, who could do this?" Kevin asked out loud.

"If I knew, I wouldn't be calling you," I replied sarcastically.

"And what is that supposed to mean?"

"You should've been here. If you were here, none of this would've happened. Our kids would probably be in bed right now as we speak. But no, you're always away from the house. Doing God knows what, while I'm here taking care of the kids by myself. And now, look at the mess we're in. Someone has my fucking kids, and I don't know where they are, or if they're all right!" I shouted through the phone. I wanted Kevin to know that his presence could've prevented this from happening. From my perspective he was the reason why the kids were abducted right under my nose.

"Look, Ava, just calm down and don't do anything until I get there. I'm hopping on the next plane out of Canada. I'll be back in a few hours. When I get home, we'll figure out how to get our hands on that kind of money," Kevin assured me before ending the call.

After this conversation I collapsed on the sofa and Paulina sat next to me. All I could think about was where my babies could be and who had them? More importantly, why they wanted so much money from us? Two million was a lot of freaking money. With Kevin's flashy image and storefront businesses, it's easy to see why the kidnappers thought we had that kind of money. It wouldn't be hard to believe that the kidnappers also knew that Kevin wasn't going to be home last night, either. They somehow knew he was on a business trip in Canada, trying to secure an auto parts deal with a Canadian businessman.

What Kevin does is sell luxury cars at a storefront location. He also has an auto parts store, which is why he's trying to secure that deal in Canada. This deal could make him a lot of money and potentially allow him to open a few more stores in the area. It could definitely be a franchise opportunity, something that he's been wanting for a very long time. Now, I understand his work ethic, but when it takes time away from the family, as it always does, that's when I have a problem. Don't get me wrong, Kevin is a great provider, and he's a good father, but the constant time away from home creates this intense wedge—and chaos wreaks havoc. But hey, what can I say? I signed up for this when I said, "I do." So I guess I gotta deal with the bullshit that comes along with him.

"So, what did he say?" Paulina wanted to know.

"He said that he was going to get on the next flight out of Canada."

"So he's on his way back home?"

"He better be," I hissed, wiping the tears from my eyes with the back of my hand.

Immediately after I ended the call with Kevin, I called my father. He is a seventy-one-year-old retiree who sits at home and watches television all day. He used to go on fishing trips regularly, but ever since my mother came down with dementia, he generally never leaves the house unless he has to run errands. When I'm not doing anything, I run the errands for him. My dad is a good man, and despite the chaotic lifestyle I used to live, he never judged or disowned me. That's why I've never lied to him, and I keep him in the loop about everything that goes on in my life. He's basically my best friend, since I don't have any siblings or close female friends. But now, I wrestled with the thought of telling him about the kids, because I didn't need him calling the cops. But I knew that I couldn't keep this type of information from him. I wouldn't be able to live with myself if something happened, and I didn't get my babies back.

"Daddy, what took you so long to answer the phone?" I asked him after he finally answered on the fifth ring.

He started chuckling. "I was letting the nurse into the house when the phone started ringing."

"Is it the same nurse?" I asked him.

"Yes, we still have Nancy. She's been good to us," he said joyfully. Then he changed the subject on me. "So, what's up? Where are the kids?"

I became serious. "Dad, I need you to come over."

"Is there something wrong?" He seemed concerned.

"I can't talk about it over the phone," I said adamantly.

He pressed me. "Are the kids all right?"

"No, they're not. Can you please come over?" I insisted, hoping he would take my direction.

"Okay, I'm on my way."

CHAPTER 2

Kevin

"**B**ABY, WHAT'S GOING ON?" TY ASKED ME AS SHE EASED HER WAY to my side of the bed.

She was wearing the fitted black lace lingerie piece I had purchased for her from the mall the day before. It was our second-year anniversary—unofficially, of course. Ty and I have secretly been together this long, and we have a three-month-old baby girl, whom I named after my mother, Annabelle. I wasn't in Canada, like Ava believed. I was actually in a town outside of Richmond, Virginia, an hour north of where Ava and I live. I met Ty Peeples on a flight from Richmond to Norfolk two years back. It was like love at first sight. She was one of the flight attendants, and we hit it off very well. We exchanged numbers, called one another, and things escalated from there.

A few months later, she invited me to her apartment, so I drove to Richmond. That night turned into a weekend-long visit and we've been together ever since. After an eighteen-month-long courtship, I moved Ty out of her apartment and into a home after I found out she was having my baby. I couldn't have her raise my child in a one-bedroom apartment. My conscience wouldn't allow that. Now, I know you're wondering, where is that same level of conscience when it pertains to Ava? Does she know about my secret life here? The answer is a resounding "no."

If Ava found out about Ty and the baby, she would probably try to kill me. Needless to say, I am going to do everything in my power to keep it quiet. Now, does Ty know about Ava? Of course, she does, and she's okay with it, too. Does she nag me about moving in with her full-time and leaving Ava? Of course, she does. I hear it all the time. But after I remind her about all the assets and property Ava and I have tied up together, and how it would take years and courts to divide these things up, she backs down and that gives me more time to live the lie that I'm living. All I have to say is: "Just give me a little more time to get enough money to give her a nice settlement, that way I don't have to give all the lawyers their attorney fees in divorce court. Because, otherwise, she will bankrupt me and then what will you have?" This bogus line works every time.

"Ava said someone came in and kidnapped the kids while she was asleep," I finally answered her after standing up from the bed.

"Are you serious?" she questioned me. Ty seemed baffled.

"I wouldn't joke about anything like that," I told her as I slid on my boxer briefs.

Ty sat up in bed, as if gathering her thoughts. "So, when did this happen?"

"She's not sure. Ava said that she just found the ransom note a few minutes ago. According to her, she went to bed around midnight, so it happened after she fell asleep," I explained.

"Has she called the cops yet?"

"No."

"Why not?"

"Because the kidnappers told her not to."

"Of course, they're gonna do that, but I would call the cops anyway," Ty protested.

"No, I told her to wait until I get there," I said while slipping on a T-shirt.

Ty pressed me. "Kev, I don't think that's a good idea."

"Well, right now, we're gonna do as the kidnappers say, until I say otherwise," I retorted. The fact that Ty was pressing me about children that I had with another woman was getting underneath my skin. She needed to know that I can handle this on my own. Ava and I would handle this the way we see fit.

Ty changed her tone. "Don't you guys have a nanny?"

"Yes, Paulina," I answered her.

She began to probe me again. "Was she there?"

I let out a long sigh. "Yeah, she was there."

"And she didn't hear anything?" Ty questioned. She seemed suspicious of Paulina.

"She said she didn't."

"I don't know, Kev. That seems fishy to me. I mean, she could've set the whole thing up. Stuff like that happens all the time."

"No, Paulina isn't like that. She's like family. The kids look at her like their grandmother. She's been with us for years." I was quick to refute the insinuation. My blood pressure seemed like it was reaching the boiling point.

"Well, you can never be too sure, Kevin. People do all sorts of things for money. And she's been around for a while, so I'm sure she has an idea of what kind of money you're working with," Ty continued with her accusations.

Hearing all of Ty's assumptions made me furious. "Look, you don't know anything about Paulina. So shut the hell up!" I roared, and dashed out of the room.

I thought Ty was going to give me back talk, but she didn't utter a word. I was shocked, to say the least. I guess she was dumbfounded that I would go off on her like I did. I had never spoken to her like that before. I knew she was probably caught off guard about it. To avoid any further conflict, I got dressed and immediately grabbed my things. On my way out of the house, I kissed my baby, and I told Ty not to worry about it. I assured her

that I'd call her after I got home, when I knew more information. She walked me to my car and then I left.

I stopped to get something to eat at a diner. I needed to kill
some time so it looked like I was flying home from Canada.
Luckily, the drive back to Tidewater took two hours, because
there was a traffic accident on the way. When I finally arrived
home, I felt a sense of coldness when I walked through the front
door. I could instantly tell that something was wrong. Something was missing, because my children always greeted me when
I walked through the front door. But today that didn't happen—
and that felt strange. I dropped my luggage on the floor of the
foyer and searched for my wife. I found her in the living room,
lying on the sofa in a fetal position, her face saturated with tears.

Paulina looked up and saw me standing there and announced
to Ava that I was home. "Look, darling, your husband is here."
But it seemed as though Ava was in no shape to switch her
"PAIN button" off and turn her focus toward me.

Consumed with so many thoughts and emotions, I just stood
there, feeling flustered. For a few moments I couldn't tell you if
I was coming or going. Standing there in front of my wife,
watching her unravel before my eyes, and trying to figure out
where the fuck my kids were, was becoming too much for me.
Thank God for my nanny and housekeeper, Paulina. Seeing the
Mexican woman console Ava in her motherly way was helping
me in a big way. I don't know what we'd do if we didn't have
Paulina. She has been with us for about eight years now. She's
more like a mother to Ava and me, and a grandmother to the kids.
I knew this tragedy was hurting her just as much as it was killing us.

"It's going to be all right, love. They will be returned to us,
safe and sound," she assured Ava as she cradled her into her
arms, rocking her back and forth on the sofa. Tears poured
from Ava's eyes uncontrollably. Her face was drenched, turning
the color of her skin a dark pink.

16

"But what if whoever has them is mistreating them?" Ava cried.

Paulina gripped Ava tighter and rubbed her back in a circular motion. "No, we're gonna think positive and believe that whoever has them is taking good care of them. And that they will return them as soon as you guys come up with the money and hand it over to them," Paulina replied.

"I told you what Kevin said, we don't have two million dollars," Ava roared back. I heard the hurt and anger in her voice. She was placing the blame on me.

I corrected her immediately. "I said that I don't have it on hand."

Without warning she broke away from Paulina's embrace, shot up from the chair, and stormed toward me. "What the fuck is the difference? On hand? Or in your possession?" she shouted.

I could tell that she wanted clarity. As badly as I wanted to tell her the truth, I couldn't. I couldn't tell her that money was tight and what little bit I had was tied up in bad investments. She wouldn't understand. Hell, I wouldn't understand if the shoe was on the other foot. A year ago, I was worth fifteen million dollars. Today I have a company that's only worth about 1.2 million—if I were to liquidate it. That's it. Most of that money belongs to one of my private investors. The home we live in is owned by my company and the cars we're driving are leased, so there's no money there. With the $560,000 I have in the bank and $200,000 I have in our home safe, that makes us about $1,240,000 short in cash. I know it's sad, but it's true.

"Look, don't worry. I'm gonna work something out," I finally said, trying to buy myself some time because I really didn't know what else to say.

"Tell me, how are you going to work it out, Kevin? I need to know what you're going to do so that we can get our kids back!" Ava roared once more.

This time it seemed like the ceiling shook. I had to admit that

Ava was a firecracker. When I met her, she was a professional car thief who worked for my best friend, Nick. They were lovers before he went to prison. While he was there serving time, Ava and I started spending a lot of time together and we ended up falling helplessly in love with one another. I guess she grew tired of my best friend's wild, thug lifestyle and decided that she wanted a guy like me who had legitimate money coming in and wasn't rough around the edges. Someone who was well respected in the community. You know, someone she could settle down with and have a family.

Once I showed her there was more to life than stealing cars, by spending long nights on the phone with her, listening to her tell me about all of her aspirations and dreams, I realized early on that all she wanted was for someone to listen to her. Not too long after that, I found out that she liked being held at night, too. And when I started cooking for her, she fell for me—hook, line, and sinker. We were so crazy in love. These days it seems that her love has shifted toward our kids. They're her world and nothing else matters. That's why I know it's killing her that they're gone. I just hope that I can bring them back in one piece.

"So, are you going to answer me or what?" she snapped. I could almost see the steam coming out of both ears.

"Ava, will you just give me a minute to think?" I shot back. She was applying too much pressure on me, making me feel less than a man.

"No, fuck that! We don't have a minute. Our kids have been gone, for God knows how long, and you're talking about giving you a minute? You know what? Screw you! I'm calling Nick. He'll get my babies back," Ava threatened, and whirled her body around to leave.

Before she could take a step, I grabbed her by the arm. "Like hell you will," I snarled as I applied pressure. She couldn't budge.

"Let me go, Kevin," she shouted as she tried to loosen my grip with her free hand.

Paulina stood up and tried to reason with us from where she was standing. "Please, you guys, we should not be fighting with one another. We've got to come together and figure out a way to get our babies back. All that other mess needs to go out of the window."

Before I could give my rebuttal, my cell phone rang. I grabbed my cell phone from my pants pocket and realized that I had to take this call, so I released Ava's arm and exited the room. I heard her yelling obscenities at me as I headed into the garage.

"Hello," I said after answering the call on the third ring.

"Hey, Kev, what's up?" I heard my best friend, Nick, say. "Hey, man, I'm just calling to check up on you."

"Man, I ain't too good right now," I said gravely.

"Tell 'im what's going on!" Ava shouted from the other room.

"I will," I replied, shouting loud enough so she could hear my response.

"Yo, dude, what's good?" Nick wanted to know. He seemed concerned.

I took a deep breath and sighed. "Somebody took my kids, man."

"What do you mean by that?" Nick asked. He didn't seem to understand what I was saying.

"Somebody came to my house last night, while I was out of town and Ava was asleep, and kidnapped my kids, Nick. They stole my fucking kids right from underneath our noses, man."

"How do you know that?"

"Because my kids aren't here, and the kidnappers left a ransom note behind."

"What are they asking for?"

"They're asking for two million, Nick."

"Have you called the cops?"

"No, they warned us not to."

"How long you got?"

"To pay them?"

"Yeah."

"The note says seventy-two hours. That means that we have until Saturday."

"Oh, shit!"

"Yeah, I know."

"You got it?"

"Nah, I don't."

"What do you mean, you don't?"

"Nick, I'm tapped out," I whispered. I couldn't afford to let Ava hear what I was saying.

"What do you mean, you're tapped out? How much do you have?"

"As far as cash?"

"Yeah."

"Not even a million."

"Damn, man, what happened to all of your money?"

"You know I just bought the house for Ty and the baby?"

"Yeah."

"Okay, and the rest of it is tied up in the business."

"So I guess that means it's gonna be a long shot before I get a return on the money I've invested in you?" Nick asked point-blank.

"Come on now, Nick, you know I've been working day and night trying to secure this auto parts deal to get you your money back. Now that this has come up, I'm really fucked."

"So, what are you going to do?"

"I was hoping I could get you to help me."

"I'm sorry, but I don't have it, either."

"Come on, Nick, I need you, man. My kids are gone and you're the only person I can go to. I have nowhere else to go."

Nick sighed. "Kev, I wish I could help you, but I'm dead in the water."

"How is that, and you got all of them motherfucking cars over there waiting to get picked up?" I instantly became enraged and shouted through the phone. I knew Nick was bullshitting me. That nigga had plenty of fucking money. I just seen him counting over five million, using a cash machine just the other day.

"Yo, dude, who the fuck you think you're talking to? I don't owe you a motherfucking thing, remember that!" he screamed back at me. He wasn't backing down.

"Listen, man, I'm sorry. I'm just in a bad way right now, and you're the only person I can go to. I don't know anyone else I can get that kind of money from. And you know I wouldn't ask you if I really didn't need it. My children's lives are at stake. If I don't come up with this money, the kidnappers will kill them."

"You know if I had it, I would give it to you," Nick said, but I knew he was lying to me. He was holding out on me, and I couldn't figure out why, especially in a time like this. I would do it for him in a heartbeat. My children's lives were in danger and he was acting like he didn't care.

"So you're saying you can't help me?"

"I'm just saying that I don't have the money," Nick replied, and then he fell silent.

I stood there with the phone in my hand, not knowing what to say next. Then he opened his mouth and spoke again. "I could probably come up with the money if you can convince Ava to do a run for me."

Hearing this request come out of his mouth and blatantly disrespect me by asking me to convince my wife to do another job for him was mind-blowing. The job he was referring to had something to do with lifting cars. I would rather die first before I let my wife get back into that game. That part of her life was over, and I refused to let her get back into it, especially at a time like this. I couldn't afford to have her out there stealing cars for her ex-lover just so we could get up the money to get our kids back from the kidnappers.

"Absolutely not, Nick. Are you out of your freaking mind? I could never convince her to do that. Not for nothing in the world," I told him. I said it with so much anger, I wanted him to hear how appalled I was by the thought of it.

"Convince me to do what?" Ava asked. I swear, her voice came from out of nowhere.

I turned around and faced her. "I'll talk to you about it later," I said, trying to brush her off.

"No, I want to hear it now," she said adamantly. She wasn't backing off.

I stood my ground. "I said, I'll talk to you about it later."

"Are you still talking to Nick?" She changed the question and reached for my phone and snatched it out of my hand. I tried to grab it back from her, but she was too quick and leapt from where I was standing to the entryway of the room.

"Nick, what is going on? What is Kevin talking about?" she abruptly asked him.

I couldn't hear what Nick was saying, but I had already had the conversation with him, so I knew what he was telling her. Ava slowly turned around and faced me. When I saw her facial expression, it gave me a clear indication as to how she was feeling about what Nick was saying to her. Three seconds in, her facial expression began to sour. "But, Nick, you know I'm not into that life anymore . . ." She began to speak, but then she fell silent.

That's when Nick took back over the conversation. I knew that Nick was doing whatever he could to convince her otherwise.

So she stood there for a few minutes and then she said, "I'm sorry, Nick, but I can't, especially right now. I mean, my children need me, and I can't jeopardize putting myself in harm's way when the objective is to get my children back. I mean, couldn't we work something else out? Come on now, at least for old times' sake?" she begged him.

I could tell that she was grasping for straws at this point. And Nick was making it very difficult for us. I mean, he already shut the door on me. Let's see how Ava's way panned out.

When I noticed her shaking her head back and forth, as if getting annoyed, I knew that this conversation wasn't going her way. I also knew that things weren't looking good for us, either. And then it happened: less than a minute later, Ava ended her call with Nick.

"So, what did he say?" I wondered aloud as she walked toward me, extending my phone in my direction.

"He said that he doesn't have the money to lend us. But if I could do two jobs for him, he'll be able to give us the rest of the money we need to get the kids back."

"You're not gonna do it, right?"

Ava sighed heavily and handed me my cell phone. "What other choice do we have, Kev?"

"We have other choices," I told her after taking my phone back from her, and I started walking out of the room. She followed me.

"And what choices are those? We have less than two and a half days to get our babies back and you don't have the slightest idea where to get the rest of the money we need," Ava shouted from behind.

"I'm gonna figure it out."

"But we don't have time for that, Kevin."

I stopped in my tracks and turned to face Ava. "Sounds like you wanna do the job," I pointed out, giving her a facial gesture that I was not happy.

"If you got a better idea, then I step out of your way," she replied.

"Do you realize how stupid you sound right now?" I snapped.

"I couldn't care less how stupid I sound right now, Kevin. I'm a way maker, and at least I have a plan," she struck back.

"What if you get caught by the cops, or the person you're stealing the car from blows your fucking head off your shoulders? Then what?"

"That's just a chance I'll have to take."

23

"Do you know how crazy that sounds? You are risking your life or freedom for some fucking money that's not even a guarantee?"

"It's fucking better than what you got lined up."

"Listen, you're not doing it—and that's the end of it," I told her before storming off.

I headed back outside of my home and climbed into my car. Ava followed me and stood alongside my car door. "Where are you going?" she wanted to know.

"I'm going to my office," I told her, rolling my driver's-side window down halfway.

"So you're going to leave me here to deal with this shit by myself?"

"I'll be right back. I'm going there to see what other monies I can scramble up."

"But what if the kidnappers call?"

"Just stay calm and be nice to them. And reassure them that we're going to get them that money."

"But what if they're mean and don't want to talk to me? What if they wanna talk to you?"

"Don't worry, they will talk to you, Ava. Just be brave for them."

"But what if I screw this up?"

"Stop thinking too much about it. You're gonna be fine," I assured her, and then I drove away.

I watched her through my rearview mirror. I could tell she was a basket case and could easily unravel at any given second. Not knowing the state of the children was eating away at her slowly.

I just hoped that I could come up with this money before any harm came to my kids. I swear, I wouldn't know what to do if something bad happened to them. My world would surely end.

CHAPTER 3

Ava

WHILE I WAS MAKING MY WAY BACK INTO THE HOUSE, MY FATHER drove up and parked on my driveway. I turned around and walked up to his car to greet him. I even held the door open when he climbed out of the car.

"Tell me, what's going on?" he started off after closing the driver's side. There was major concern and trepidation written all over his face.

I grabbed him by the hand and led him into the house. As soon as we entered the foyer, I stood there before him and said, "You've gotta promise me that you will let me handle what I am about to tell you."

He hesitated for a few seconds and then asked, "Ava, what is this all about?" He became agitated.

I wouldn't let up. "You've gotta promise me first."

"Okay, okay. I promise. What is it?"

"You promise you won't call the cops?"

"Call the cops! Ava, what is going on?" His voice hit a high pitch.

I grabbed him by the hand. "Dad, I need you to calm down."

"Not until you tell me what's going on," he demanded. His pitch was the same.

"Dad, the kids were kidnapped last night after Paulina and I went to bed . . ."

My dad snatched his hand away from me and stormed down the hallway. Then angling around a corner, and through the entryway to my living room, he shouted, "Kammy . . . Little Kevin!"

I started off behind him. "Dad, they're not here!" I shouted, right before suddenly breaking down in tears as he followed me into the open room.

He turned around and faced me. "How do you know that they were kidnapped?"

"Because I got a ransom note and they're asking for two million dollars."

"Two million!" he barked. He was lit with fury. "Oh no, you've gotta call the police." He was adamant.

"No, Dad, we can't." I sobbed louder, tears springing from my eyes like a running faucet. "They said that if we called the cops, I won't ever see my kids again." I tried to explain the instructions I'd been given, but I already knew that my father wouldn't understand, and it was cutting me deep that he was hurting.

"So, what are you going to do? And what is Kevin saying about all of this?"

"Kevin is going to the office to see how much money we have so we can get my babies back," I told him.

"So he's okay with not calling the cops?"

"Yes," I replied.

"But what if you come up with the money and they still don't return our babies?"

"They will, Dad," I replied confidently as I swiped a flow of tears from my cheeks.

"But what if they don't?" my dad spoke over me, his words full of doubt.

"I've gotta remain optimistic, Dad. I gotta think positive, and that's what I'm gonna hold on to."

My dad was starting to realize my pain and started easing up a bit. "Are you sure you're doing the right thing?" he asked me as calmly as he could. It was very evident that he wanted clarification.

"Right now, I can't afford pissing those guys off and losing my babies in the process, so just trust me on this one."

I could tell that he was still wrestling with the idea of going along with my plan, but after mulling it over for a bit, he finally conceded.

"Okay, I'm gonna go along with this, but please don't make me regret it," he finally said.

I forced a smile on my washed-out face. "Thank you, Dad. I appreciate it."

"So, out of curiosity, how much money have you come up with so far?" he wanted to know.

"I'm not sure. Kevin has his money tied up in a lot of business ventures, so there's not a lot lying around. But I'm thinking he may be able to come up with close to a million."

"What are you going to do about the rest?"

"I'm trying to figure that out right now."

"Your mama and I may have about two hundred thousand put away from our retirement. You can have all of it."

"Thank you, Daddy. I appreciate it," I said, feeling relieved. I truly appreciated that my dad would offer me all of his retirement money to get my kids back. Under any other circumstances I would not have taken it. But I was desperate right now, and every dollar I got would help to get me one step closer to bringing my kids home.

With his eyebrows furrowed with worry, my dad managed to hug me tight and told me everything would be all right. "How do you want me to get this money to you?" he asked after releasing me from his embrace.

"I'm gonna need it in cash. But I don't know if your bank is going to let you take out all of that money from your account at one time."

"They have no choice. It's mine."

"Dad, they're gonna give you a hard time. One of those bank tellers will be bound to call the cops, because they're gonna think someone is making you withdraw all of your money out of the bank, and I don't need that kind of heat," I said, still sobbing, but doing it lightly.

My dad's face softened as he grabbed my hand gently. He hated to see me cry. He still thought of me as his little girl, no matter how old I got. "Okay, I'll walk to the beat of your drum. Just let me know what I need to do, and I'll do it," he swore.

My dad stuck around for a couple of hours. He would've stayed longer, but he had to go and tend to my mother. He did say that he'd be around to check on me later. I made him promise not to mention this to anyone. He gave me his word that he wouldn't.

After my dad left, I noticed that Kevin's things were left by the front door. I asked Paulina if she could take Kevin's bags to the bedroom and unpack them. She agreed and carried on as instructed. I went into the kitchen to get something to drink, and then the house phone rang. I rushed to the island, where the cordless phone was, and answered it on the second ring.

"Hello," I said.

"Hi, is this Mrs. Frost?" the caller asked.

"Yes, this is she."

"Hi, this is Mr. Heights, school administrator from the attendance office at Potomac Elementary School, calling because we've noticed that Kammy and Kevin weren't in school today. Is there a reason why?" he asked.

Caught off guard by this man's call, I was stumped by his question. I didn't know whether to lie and say that my kids were sick, or to burst into tears and tell him they were gone without a trace. Kidnapped by some strangers and I didn't have any idea where they could be. But then I figured if I did, that would open up a whole new can of worms and he could call the cops, and everything would go downhill from there. That would go against everything the kidnappers told me to do and not to do.

"Yes, um, they're here. And, um, they're in bed," I finally said, my heart racing at a rapid speed. It felt like my heart was going to take a plunge into the pit of my stomach.

"Are they ill?" he pressed me.

"Um, yes, sir, they're sick." My mind continued to race uncontrollably.

"It isn't Covid, is it?" he pressed me some more. I swear, this man was getting underneath my skin.

"No, they both woke up saying that their stomach was aching. I figured it had to do with something they ate the previous night, and they may have a stomach virus, so I decided to keep them home so I could monitor them," I explained.

"Oh, okay. Well, I'll go ahead and make a note of that. If this continues till tomorrow, please make sure you give us a call in the morning. Our office opens at eight a.m."

"Sure will. And thanks for calling."

"No, thank you," he said, and then we both ended the call.

As soon as I placed the phone back on the island in the kitchen, through my peripheral vision I noticed Paulina come up from behind me, so I turned and looked over my shoulder. She gave me an odd look and then held up something in her hand. I turned around and zoomed in on what she was holding. It was a picture, so I took it out of her hand. As soon as I took one look at it, my heart hit the floor like a ton of bricks. My mouth widened as I stared at the photo of Kevin, with a woman lying in a hospital bed with a newborn baby in her arms. My heart started racing as I wondered, who could this woman be?

I looked up at Paulina, who was waiting for my reaction, and said, "Where did you find this?"

"In Mr. Frost's toiletry bag. And it wasn't hidden. When I opened the bag to take his things out of it, it looked to me like it had been placed there," she insisted.

Instantly my heart began to ache while I tried to process this photo and everything Paulina was telling me. "So you think that whoever this woman is, she placed this photo in his bag?"

"Yes, ma'am, I do."

"Do you think that this is his baby?"

"There's a possibility that it is."

Crushed by Paulina's words, I took my right hand and covered my eyes with it. Then I moved the palm of my hand across my forehead and then around to the right temple and began to massage it. The thought of my husband having an affair, and having a baby on me, especially right now, was becoming agonizing. I left Nick for cheating on me; now I was being forced to deal with Kevin doing the same, and possibly having a baby on top of that. That's a bit much.

"So, what are you going to do? Are you going to confront him?" Paulina asked.

"Of course, I am. I'm going to call that bastard now," I said through clenched teeth. I was seething right now. How deceitful can one man be? All the lies and dishonesty were downright hurtful; he had some explaining to do.

I grabbed the cordless phone again and began to dial Kevin's number. Immediately after it started ringing, I began rehearsing in my mind what I was going to say to him. And then it hit me that it would be better if I FaceTimed him. That way I could look at him when I asked him about this woman and child. I hurried up and disconnected the call, then went to grab my cell phone from where it was lying around in the living room. Paulina was down on my heels and she stood there from the time I dialed Kevin's number again, up until the time he answered. I could see that he was still driving, because he'd occasionally look at me and then he would turn his eyes toward the road in front of him.

"What happened since I left?" he immediately asked. He saw the hurt in my eyes, and he could sense that it was something other than the situation dealing with our kids. So I held up the photo of him, the woman, and the baby in plain view so that he could see it clearly.

"Who is this, Kevin?" I didn't hesitate to ask.

"Where did you get that?" was his rebuttal. I could tell that he didn't want to answer my question.

"I got it out of your hygiene bag. Now tell me, who is this woman? And then I want you to tell me if this is your baby," I continued.

"Let me call you when I get to the office."

"No, fuck that, Kevin. Answer me right now!" I screamed into the phone. "Who is this fucking lady, and is this your baby?" I wasn't letting up.

He wouldn't look at me, he kept his eyes on the road, and this infuriated me even more. "Kevin, answer me right now. Who are these fucking people in this picture?" I shouted at the top of my voice. Tears even started falling from my eyes, because at this point I had already had the answers to my question. He had made it painfully obvious who these people were. But it was just something inside of me that wanted him to utter the words from his mouth. "Tell me, Kevin, is that your baby?" I shouted once again.

He turned and faced his phone and said, "Yes, Ava, that's my baby."

I swear, at that very moment it felt like someone had stabbed me in the gut with a butcher's knife. The imaginary blow to my stomach literally took the wind out of me and I gasped for air. Before I could utter another word, Kevin abruptly told me he would call me back and then he ended the call.

"Wait, you better not hang up on me!" my voice screeched, but it was too late, he was gone. I dialed his number again, but it wouldn't connect, so I knew he had turned it off. I was both heartbroken and furious. So much so, I became lightheaded and my knees started buckling. Paulina noticed this and insisted that I take a seat on the sofa. After I did, she sat down next to me. I buried my head in her chest and let out a floodgate of tears.

"Paulina, can you believe this? He went out there and had an affair and fathered another baby. How could he do this to me? I thought that he loved me!" I sobbed.

"Look, Ava, now isn't the time to be crying over a man. They come a dime a dozen. Your babies need you right now and they're counting on you to come up with that money for their safe return. So pull yourself together and let's figure out how we're gonna get our babies back," Paulina instructed me in a stoic fashion.

I sat up, looked into her eyes, and saw how serious she was. Paulina has never gotten involved with any of my or Kevin's disputes. So when she spoke up just now, I knew her words were coming from the heart, and I listened. "You're right. Screw him. I've gotta figure out how to get my babies back," I agreed, using the back of my hands to wipe the tears away from my eyes.

"That's my girl," Paulina said, cheering me on.

I held my phone up in my hand and dialed Nick's cell phone number. After it rang three times, he answered.

"Hello," he said.

"Hey, this is Ava."

"Hey, Ava, what's up? Had a change of heart?" he asked me.

"Yes, I have."

"Wanna stop by my place?"

"I'm on my way," I told him, and then I ended the call.

CHAPTER 4

Kevin

I KNEW TY PUT THAT FUCKING PICTURE OF HER, ME, AND THE BABY IN my bag before I left her house this morning, and now she's got some fucking explaining to do.

"Hi, baby," she said after answering my FaceTime call.

"You know you did some foul shit, right?" I didn't hesitate to say.

"What are you talking about?" she replied, giving off a surprised expression.

"Ty, don't play games with me. You know what I'm talking about."

"No, I don't." She continued to pretend as if she didn't know what I was talking about. But I knew her like the back of my hand. I knew when she was lying, and the dead giveaway was the fact that she would avoid eye contact with me and act as if something else had her attention. This time it happened to be the button she was tampering with on her shirt.

"Leave your shirt alone and look at me," I snapped. She was beginning to irritate the hell out of me.

"I'm looking at you," she replied after she had sucked her teeth and rolled her eyes.

"Why did you sneak that picture of you, me, and the baby into my bag before I left the house this morning?" I asked her flat out. I gave her a stern look.

She turned her face, like something else had gotten her attention.

"Ty, answer me," I demanded.

She gave me a guilty look. "Okay, I slipped it in your bag. But I didn't mean for her to find it. I only put it there so that you could think about us, despite everything that's going on with your other kids. You know, like a pick-me-up," she explained. The innocent look she displayed on her face changed my mood that instant. I couldn't be mad at her anymore. I knew she meant well.

"It's okay," I told her.

"What did she say?" she wanted to know.

"What do you mean, what did she say? She wanted to know who you and the baby were."

"What did you tell her?"

"I told her the truth."

"What did she say?" Ty pressed me more.

"She started screaming and I hung up."

"So you weren't home?"

"No, she found the picture after I left the house and Face-Timed me."

"Was she crying?"

"No, she started off calm and then she started screaming."

"So, what do you think she's going to do?"

"I don't know."

"Think she's going to ask for a divorce?"

"Look, Ty, I can't talk about that right now."

"Why not? I mean, the cat's out of the bag now."

"Because I've gotta focus on my kids. I've gotta figure out how to get them back. So talking about getting a divorce is the furthest thing from my mind right now."

"Did you tell her what our daughter's name was?"

"The conversation didn't get that far."

Ty let out a long sigh. "So you're on your way to your office?"

"Yes."

"Why aren't you at the house?"

"Because I've gotta figure out how to come up with this money."

"And you can't do that at your house?"

"No, I've got all my account records, ledgers, and some cash at the office. Plus, I need somewhere quiet so I can think more clearly. Someplace I can make calls without being interrupted."

"Well, you know the conversation is going to come back up again about me and the baby. So, are you going to be ready?"

"Ty, I don't wanna talk about that right now."

"I'm only trying to prepare you because it's coming. Does she know you're on your way to the office?"

"Yeah."

"Then it wouldn't surprise me if she doesn't show up there and confront you with it."

"She's not going to leave the house."

"Well, then, she's definitely going to confront you when you go back home. She's going to be waiting for you to come right through that door, and—"

"Look, let me call you back," I interrupted her. I was growing tired of hearing her talk about this situation with her and the baby.

"All right," she replied, and disconnected the call right before I did.

CHAPTER 5

Ty

Yep, I HUNG UP ON KEVIN BEFORE HE GOT THE CHANCE TO HANG the phone up on me. I mean, how dare he cut me off in mid-sentence? Shit, I was just trying to help him figure out how to talk about the situation when Ava brings it back up to him. It's not going away, and neither are we. My baby and I are here to stay, and Ava will find out soon enough.

But in the meantime I'm gonna get my homegirl Whitney and bring her up to speed. She'd be pleased to know that the wife now knows about me and the baby.

"Whitney, you up?" I asked after she answered her phone.

"Yeah, what's up?"

"She knows," I said.

"Who?"

"Kevin's wife."

"No fucking way!"

"Yes, way!"

"When did she find out?"

"Just a few minutes ago. Kevin just called and told me."

"So he told her?"

"No, see, what happened was, when he left this morning to go back home, I slid a picture of me, him, and the baby in one of his carry-on bags. She found it and confronted him."

Whitney chuckled. "Slick move!"

"I know, right?"

"So, what did she say?"

"Well, he wasn't home when she found the picture, so she called him and asked him about it over the phone. And whatever she said, he didn't deny it."

"Damn, I would've loved to have been able to eavesdrop on that conversation," Whitney said.

"Me too," I agreed.

"So, how do you feel about it?"

"About her knowing?"

"Yeah."

"I feel good. Shit, you know how long I've been holding my breath about that. Who knows how long it was going to take him to tell her about us?"

"Well, she knows about y'all now. So you think she's going to divorce him?"

"I asked him the same question, but he didn't want to talk about it."

"What do you think?"

"Well, if it was me, I would be done with his ass. I mean, it's one thing to cheat, but then to bring a baby into it, that is a whole other ballgame," I answered.

"Yeah, I'm with you. I'd bounce on his ass, too. But it wouldn't surprise me if she sticks around. You know, women these days will try to hold on to a man even when they know that nigga don't want them. I seen it a few times," Whitney said, and then she changed the subject. "Where's the baby?"

"She's asleep. I just fed her and laid her down about fifteen minutes ago."

"She still keeping you up all night?"

"Not all night. She'll sleep from nine o'clock at night until two in the morning. And then she'll stay up till about four a.m. and sleep until about eight a.m."

"That's not bad."

"I know. I remember when she used to sleep all day and stay up all night. That shit used to drive me crazy."

"How is Kevin when he's there with you guys?"

"He's really good with her. During the nights he's here, he never lets me get out of bed at night when she wakes up. He does all the diaper changing and bottle making. He feeds her and bathes her, too."

"Sounds like your little angel is a daddy's girl already."

"Yeah, it seems that way. That's why I can't wait until he ends that situation over there and comes here full-time. Annabelle is going to need her dad."

"I get it. I wouldn't know what to do if Darius had to spend half of his time here and the other fifty percent of his time somewhere else. Girl, I would lose it," Whitney admitted.

"Yeah, I've been wondering how I've lasted this long."

"Well, don't worry. She knows about you and the baby now. Maybe it won't be long before the ink is dry on the divorce papers and he's living in that house with you."

I let out a long sigh. "I can't wait."

CHAPTER 6

Ava

I CRIED THE ENTIRE DRIVE TO NICK'S CAR SHOP, THINKING ABOUT THE photo with Kevin, his mistress, and that fucking bastard baby. That baby had to be at least a couple of months old. So, by my estimation, he had to be messing around with that chick for at least a year now, if not more. From the looks of the photo, they appeared like a cozy little family, and they looked happy. If he wasn't my husband, I would think she was the wife, and that baby was the only child he had. But no, that motherfucker had another family. Apparently, the family he started out with—me and his two children—weren't enough for him anymore. Now he was playing house with some other bitch. How fucking dare he!

It was a good thing God had him leave the house when he did, because I swear, I would've tried to stab him with a knife if he was in front of me when I confronted him about that picture. Our house would've been turned into a bloodbath. And I can't have that, especially with the situation going on with my children. I've got to push through the pain I'm feeling now and think about them. I need to have a clear head and focus on them, which was why I had to leave the house. I instructed

Paulina to call me if anything happened while I was gone. As far as the house phone was concerned, I forwarded all calls that would come into the house to my cell phone. This way I wouldn't miss the kidnappers if they decided to call.

When I reached Nick's place, one of his mechanics opened the side warehouse door and let me in. Then he escorted me to Nick's office. Nick was sitting behind his desk on the phone when I walked in. His face lit up like a Christmas tree when he laid eyes on me. "Let me call you back," he told the caller, and ended his call abruptly.

Nick stood up from his desk and walked around it. I got a look at him and for a moment there I lost my train of thought. That's just how good he looked. See, Nick had a gorgeous body. He was physically fit, from head to toe. He had the perfect height, tight abs, hairless chest, perfectly measured pecs, protruding arms—an overall-nice physique. You name it, this brother had it all. He was eye candy for sure, and I wasn't the only girl who noticed it, either.

Nick knew he looked good. How could he not, when he was constantly being reminded by other women? That's the reason why I left his rotten ass in jail in the first place. He was a womanizer. Adding insult to injury, the same women who used to compliment him on the daily made it a regular practice to throw themselves at him. One cheating episode turned into another, and then it became a repeating offense for him, and of course I had to leave. Now, then, don't get me wrong. I missed the times we used to have because Nick was a very generous man and I knew that he loved me, but the cheating was a dealbreaker for me, so I never looked back.

"Come, give me a hug," he insisted as he extended his arms out to me.

I leaned in, allowing him to cradle me in his arms. I have to admit that it felt damn good, especially with all this pain I was feeling at the moment. I honestly didn't want him to let go. But I needed to remain focused, so I broke away from his embrace.

"Thanks for everything," I said after stepping back away from him.

"Don't mention it. Come on, take a seat," he instructed as he pointed to a chair near his desk.

I sat down and crossed my legs.

"Want something to drink? Coffee? Bottle of water?"

"No, I'm good," I answered.

He took a seat in the chair next to me and faced me. "So fill me in," he encouraged me.

I took a deep breath and exhaled, because it was a lot to deal with. After I got a clear snapshot of what I was going to say, I opened up the floodgates. "As Kevin mentioned earlier, we've gotta come up with two million dollars and have less than seventy-two hours to do it. I don't know who the kidnappers are. I don't know when they entered my home. And I don't know if my kids are okay. All I know is that I've gotta come up with this money or else I'm not ever gonna see my kids again."

"Where is Kevin?"

"Don't even mention his name," I said through clenched teeth.

Surprised by my outburst, Nick replied, "Did I miss something?"

"Did you know that he was cheating on me?" I asked him abruptly.

"No, I didn't."

Surprised by his answer, I said, "Come on now, Nick, don't lie to me. You guys are best fucking friends. You know everything about him."

Nick gave me a look, one that I knew perfectly well. It was the look of *Yeah, I know, but it ain't my place to say.* But I wasn't having it. He was going to give up the goods. I mean, that's the least he could do, considering our former relationship. "So you do know about that bitch?" I gritted. "And I bet you know about the baby, too?" I continued as I leaned my upper body toward him.

He turned his head and looked at me sideways.

"Spill it, Nick. I mean, I already know. Just tell me what the ho's name is?"

"Ty," he finally said.

"Ty," I repeated.

"Yeah, her name is Ty."

"How long has he been with this bitch?" I screeched.

"I don't know. Maybe two years now, I guess. Maybe less. Maybe more. I don't know."

"Where does she live?" I probed him. I needed more answers.

"She's from Richmond."

"So this nigga drives all the way to Richmond to see this ho?"

"Yeah, I guess."

"And that's his baby, too, huh?"

"Yep."

"So, how old is this baby?"

"I don't know for sure. Maybe a couple of months."

"Is it a girl or a boy?"

"It's a girl."

"What's her name?"

"He named her after his mother."

I chuckled loudly out of rage. "He named that baby Anna-belle?"

Nick confirmed by nodding his head.

"How fucking dare him? That motherfucker!" I roared, biting down on my bottom lip. I swear, if that bastard was in front of me, I would've done some damage to his face. Inflicting pain would've soothed me for the moment. "After all I've done for him, this is how he repays me? He goes out there and has an affair and then gets the bitch pregnant? I mean, usually, men go out and cheat, but they don't get attached to the other women. They fuck 'em and then move on to the next. But this fool did. It almost makes me think that he really loves and wants to be with her," I surmised, then looked at Nick and hoped he would give me some clarity.

Nick reluctantly gave me that look again and that's when I knew. I slumped my head over and the pain I was feeling engulfed me. Tears formed in my eyes, and I started sobbing all over again. Nick got out of his chair and threw his arms around me. He held me tight and insisted that everything would be all right.

"Ava, you've got to pull yourself together. You can't let this break you down. We've got shit to do so we can get your kids back," he reminded me.

I lifted my head and looked at him through my glassy eyes. "You're gonna help me?" I wondered aloud.

"Of course, I am," he assured me.

I instantly felt a glimmer of hope. Nick was the type of guy who always made shit happen. He was a man of ideas, resources, and connections. If he didn't know something, his answer was a quick phone call away. "Come on, let's get these two jobs done so that we can get this money," he added. Then he stood up and grabbed two photos from his top desk drawer.

"Let me show you something," Nick said as he laid both photos down on top of his desk.

I got up from my chair and leaned over his desk. I zoomed in on the photos and saw two different cars. At the bottom of the photos was detailed information about them. See, I was familiar with this. This was called the spec sheet and not everyone can get them. Not only do they have all the information there is to know about the car, but it also lists how many were made, who the owners of them are, and how much was paid for each one. You can only get this document through the black market.

"When did you get this?" I asked Nick.

"Two days ago," he answered.

I looked at the first photo and it was an image of a British Marque Rolls-Royce. They called it the Boat Tail Coachbuild Edition. It was unveiled last year, and its price tag was a whopping $28,000,000. According to the specs, there were only two manufactured and purchased. It was rumored that one of them had been purchased by Jay-Z and Beyoncé, and the other one belonged to a billionaire real estate mogul out in New York, who just recently bought it, and it was going to be shipped via cargo freight container through the Port of Norfolk. After reading that tidbit of information, something didn't seem right to me. So I looked up from the paper. "This car comes in tomorrow night."

"I know," Nick confirmed.

"Well, answer this . . ."

"Shoot."

"Why would this car come through the Norfolk terminal, when the buyer is from New York? Why wouldn't it go through one of the New York ports?" I asked him.

"Because the owner of it wanted it sooner than any of the freight companies in the New York terminal could get it shipped to him. So he went with the next best thing. Get it shipped to Norfolk, have it put on the back of a truck, and then driven the rest of the way to New York. If he would've waited to get it in through the New York ports, he'd have to wait an additional two months because of how backlogged the container ships are with the loads they already have. So, you see, having it come into Norfolk, Virginia, was his best option."

"And that's where we come in?"

"Exactly."

"You do know that he's going to have security all over that car? I mean, he paid twenty-eight million dollars for it."

"Don't worry about that. I've got a team that's going to get them right out of the way," Nick revealed.

"So, what do you need me for?"

"To drive it from one container to the next."

"But that's easy. You can get anyone to do that."

"I can't risk them damaging it in any way. Plus, where I need it to go would be on the other side of the terminal, and I need it done without anyone seeing it."

"A car at that price is going to have a tracking device on it," I was quick to point out.

"Of course, it is, and you, of all people, know how to remove it."

"Do you have a map of the container and where it's located on the other side of the terminal?"

"Yes, I do," Nick assured me while turning the photo over. There on the back of it was a map of the entire Norfolk terminal. But it looked more like a grid with several markings on them. One location of the map was circled and highlighted. It was where the Rolls-Royce would be when it was taken off the ship. The other location marking was where I would need to take the car, once I had it in my possession. From the looks of it, it seemed easy. But when you're driving a car like that around an industrial terminal, it was going to stick out like a sore thumb.

"Do you know how many security drivers will be patrolling tomorrow night?" I asked Nick.

"Two."

"Do you know who they are?"

"The security company rotates their drivers on a daily basis, but don't worry, I can find out."

After Nick ran down the rest of the specifics to me concerning the Rolls, I looked at the next photo and it was a picture of a classic 1954 Mercedes-Benz W196, valued at $29,600,000. The owner of it was a billionaire who recently died. The car had been willed to one of his favorite charities in the D.C. area and it was being auctioned off to the highest bidder. The auction was going to take place in two weeks.

"When is it coming in?" I wondered aloud.

Nick pointed to the bottom of the paper. The delivery manifest date was there typed in bold letters. Estimated date of arrival: 4/12/2024.

I looked back up at Nick. "That's a day apart."

"Yep."

"That's gonna be impossible to do, once the heat comes down after the owner of the Rolls-Royce finds out that the tracker was deactivated on his car," I stressed to Nick.

"We're gonna reactivate it onto another car. By the time that car reaches its destination, we'll have both cars in our possession," Nick said confidently.

I thought about his plan for a moment, and after sorting out a few things in my mind, I felt like it was doable. I mean, it might take some tweaks here and there, but for the most part, I should be able to pull it off. But then it dawned on me how much cash he was potentially getting for these vehicles and my entrepreneurial spirit awakened in me. "How much am I making from these pickups?" I asked him.

"Whatcha want?" Nick threw the question back at me.

This was his way of negotiating with me. He never liked to throw out the first number. He always allowed the other person to do that and then he'd go low. And then he and the other person would meet somewhere in the middle. That's how he always operated.

"I want half from each car," I boldly stated.

He looked at me like I had lost my mind. "No way. I can give you a fourth of the value," he shot back.

"That's only seven million each," I protested.

"Do you know that I can get any car thief to pull that job off?" he threatened.

46

"If you could, then why am I here?"

He paused for a second and attempted to say something, but he didn't.

I scoffed. "That's what I thought. So I want half."

"I'll do a thirty-five, sixty-five split, and that's my final offer."

I thought for a moment, calculating the math, and then I agreed.

CHAPTER 7

Kevin

MY SECRETARY, MAGGIE, WALKED INTO THE OFFICE THIRTY MINutes late and I could tell she was shocked to see me sitting behind my desk. Maggie was a twenty-five-year-old college graduate who was highly recommended by one of her college professors, whom I've known for several years now. In my opinion she strongly resembles the singer Rihanna, but Ava disagrees. When she first saw her, she didn't like the idea that I had hired such a young and attractive Black girl, being that my old office assistant was a quirky, odd-dressing young girl. I could sense some insecurity when Ava came to the office; so to keep the drama down, I made Ava feel like the queen around the office when she'd come visit.

It's funny, because Maggie felt the tension sometime when Ava was around, so she tried to either kiss her ass or avoid her at all costs. "So you're back early?" were her first words.

"Yeah, I had a family emergency and had to come back."

"Is everything all right?" she asked, placing her purse and suit jacket down on her desk that was situated in a glassed-in-case office a few feet away from my office. I could see directly into her space, and she could see directly into mine.

"Everything will be fine," I told her. "But I'm going to need you to get on the phone and make a few phone calls for me."

"Okay. Just let me know whom to call," she said eagerly.

I gave her a list of customers to call who owed me money. "Put pressure on them," I stressed to her. I couldn't tell her why, but she saw the urgency in my face, so I hoped that she'd take heed.

During the first couple of hours at work, I managed to pull together $718,000. If I added that to the $560,000 I had in the bank, and the $200,000 in cash at home, I had $1,478,000. I was now $522,000 short, but what was so tragic about this was that I had less than two days now to come up with it.

Now, where the fuck was I going to get the rest of this money? Nick wouldn't lend it to me. I wouldn't be able to get it from a bank, not in this short amount of time anyway. I don't know anyone else I'd be able to borrow it from. Maybe if I called my parents, I could get a couple of thousand dollars from them. Who knows? I guessed I wouldn't know unless I gave them a call.

Unlike Ava's parents, mine weren't together. My parents divorced when I was a teenager. My mother remarried, but my dad didn't. So, first on my list to call was my mother. I couldn't admit to her what's going on with the kids, but I could tell her that I was in dire need of money and then see what she was able to lend me. Hopefully, I could come away with at least ten grand, if not more.

"Hey, Mom," I said after she answered the phone.

"Hi, baby, how are you?" she replied. She seemed excited to speak with me. It had been a few days since I had last spoken with her. She doesn't know about my new baby, but my dad does. My mom would be very disappointed by my actions, plus I know it would break her heart, so I've got to find the right time to tell her. That time isn't right now, though.

"I'm not good, Mom," I said in a low tone so that Maggie wouldn't hear me.

"What's wrong, baby?"

"I need a loan, Mom."

"What kind of loan?"

"What can you give me?" I asked vaguely. I couldn't tell her the real reason I needed the money because that would alarm her, so I tried to keep it simple.

She immediately became concerned. "Are you in any trouble?"

"No, I'm not in any trouble. I just need the money to close this major deal," I lied. This was the only thing I could think of.

"What kind of deal is it?"

Regretting that I'd told her I needed the money to close a deal, I had to feed her another lie.

"You know I'm trying to get the auto parts account, right?"

"Yeah."

"Well, in order to secure that account, I need over four hundred thousand dollars in liquid cash and I'm short fifty-thousand dollars," I told her.

"Kevin, I don't have that kind of money." Her voice hit a high pitch.

"Well, what could you give me?"

"Maybe five thousand."

"What about ten?"

"You mean ten thousand?"

"Yeah."

"Son, I don't have ten thousand dollars lying around like that. Where is your money anyway? I thought you had over a million dollars in the bank," she questioned me.

"Not anymore."

"Why don't you liquidate some of your assets?"

"If I did that, it's gonna take at least a week to receive the funds and I need the money today."

"Well, I don't have ten thousand dollars. Maybe five."

"Okay, I'll take that."

"Well, stop by and pick up the check."

"Could you wire it to me?"

"You know I'm not into all of that technology stuff. I'm old school. I write checks and that's what you're gonna get," she said adamantly.

I let out a long sigh. "All right, Mom."

"So, how is Ava?"

"She's fine."

"And the kids?"

"They're good, too."

"You know that if she was working, you wouldn't be in this situation."

"Mom, I'm not gonna do this today," I asserted. She had always been against Ava being a stay-at-home mom after the kids started going to school.

"I've worked every day since you went off to school. Your wife should be doing the same thing," she was constantly telling me.

"Okay, Mom, you got it," I interjected. "I'll be over there in about an hour to pick up the check."

"All right, see you then," she said. Then we ended the call.

Immediately after I got a clear line, I called my dad. He seemed happy to hear from me. "How are you doing, son?" he said with excitement.

"Not too good, Dad."

"Is the family all right?"

As badly as I wanted to tell him that my kids had been kidnapped and the kidnappers wanted two million dollars, I couldn't bring myself to do it. I couldn't get him involved. This was my problem, and I was going to deal with it on my own.

"Ava found out about Ty and the baby," I volunteered.

"Does she want a divorce?"

"She hasn't said it, but I know it's coming."

"Well, son, you knew this was bound to happen. You can't go out and cheat on your wife, have a baby, and expect her to want to stay married to you. I told you when I cheated on your mother, I didn't make a baby, but she put me out of the house that same night. I was forced to go to my brother's house and live there until I was able to get my own place. What was crazy about the whole thing is the lady I cheated with, I didn't even like her like that. She was just some old Jezebel I met at the bar after work."

"Well, I love Ty, and if Ava and I get a divorce, then I'm gonna marry her."

"You got it all figured out, huh?" my dad commented sarcastically.

"As best as I can. But that's not what I called you for."

"What's on your mind?"

"I need a loan."

"How much do you need?"

"Twenty thousand," I said, just throwing out a number. I knew he wasn't going to bite, but I said it anyway.

"Twenty thousand dollars?"

"Yeah."

"What makes you think I have twenty thousand dollars?"

"I don't know. I thought that maybe you had it stashed somewhere underneath your mattress," I said nonchalantly.

"Are you in some kind of trouble?"

"No, Dad, I'm not."

"So, what's wrong with your finances that you need twenty thousand dollars? I thought you were doing okay over there."

"My money is tied up in a lot of investments, and all these bills I've accumulated are starting to catch up with me."

"How much did that house you bought for Ty set you back?"

"A couple of hundred thousand."

"Does Ava know about the house?"

"Hell no. She'd kill me."

"I'm shocked she hasn't killed you already."

I let out another exasperated sigh. "Dad, can you give me the money or not?"

"What about your friend Nick? Why don't you ask him?"

"I went to him first."

"And he doesn't have it?"

"No, he doesn't."

"But I thought he had that big car shop over there, off South Military Highway."

"Yeah, he does, but his money is tied up, too."

"That's too bad."

"So, what is it gonna be, Dad?"

"I don't have twenty thousand, son. I can probably pull together seven."

"Seven grand?"

"Yeah, that's it. You know I'm living on a fixed income."

"Yeah, I know. And believe me, I appreciate it."

"Well, you know this is a loan, right?"

"Yes, Dad, I know it's a loan." After I scheduled a time to stop by his house to pick up the money, he agreed to see me later and then we ended the call.

CHAPTER 8

Little Kevin & Kammy

"I WANT MOMMY," AVA'S SEVEN-YEAR-OLD DAUGHTER, KAMMY, whined as she sat on the bed of a room that was housed in the basement.

Her nine-year-old big brother, Kevin, cradled her in his arms like a protector. "Don't worry, we're gonna see her again," he assured her confidently.

They were both dressed in their pajamas from the night before. Despite Little Kevin's confident demeanor, they both looked scared and unaware what was going to happen next.

"What if we don't?" she wondered aloud.

"But we will, so don't talk like that."

"What if they hurt us?"

"No one is going to put their hands on you. Ever," he swore to her.

"If Dad was home, he wouldn't have let those men take us out of the house. He would've used his gun on them," Kammy insisted.

"Yeah, he sure would've. But it's okay, because Mom and Dad will get us back."

"But when?"

"Soon."

"When is *soon?*"

"I don't know. But it won't be long."

"Think Mommy's crying and wondering where we are?" Kammy wanted to know.

"I'm sure she is. That's what moms do."

"What about Dad?" Kammy continued.

"I'm sure he's doing the same thing."

"What are you two talking about?" a male's voice asked after the door to the room suddenly opened.

Both children looked up and saw a man wearing a white hockey mask, clothed in all-black attire. This freaked Kammy out. She started sobbing instantly.

"Kevin, the monster man is going to hurt us!" she cried out.

Little Kevin stood up on his feet. "Don't come near us!" he shouted as he poked out his chest.

The masked man held up his hands. "I'm not here to hurt you guys. I just came in here to check on you. And to see if you're hungry," he stated.

"We're good," Little Kevin told him.

"I'm hungry," Kammy interjected.

The masked man chuckled. "Whatcha want to eat, little lady?"

"Burger and fries."

"McDonald's or Burger King?"

"McDonald's."

"Want something to drink, too?"

"Yeah."

"Whatcha want?"

"Soda."

"Any kind of sofa?"

"Sprite."

"I gotcha," he assured her, and Kammy seemed pleased. So

the masked man turned his attention toward Little Kevin. "And what about you, li'l man? You can have anything you want," the guy said kindly.

Little Kevin stood there for a second. More hesitant than ever. He didn't know whether to stand tall or give in. He was, in fact, hungry. But he didn't want to show any sign of weakness. The masked man noticed this and came at him another way, using reverse psychology. "I'll tell you what, li'l man. I'm gonna bring another hamburger, French fries, and soda. If you decide you wanna eat it, then you can eat it. A'ight?"

Little Kevin nodded as he continued to stand there boldly; his facial expression didn't change.

"A'ight, well, sit tight and I'll be right back," the man said.

"Excuse me," Kammy spoke up.

"Yeah," the man responded.

"Why are you wearing that mask?"

The man chuckled. "Because I have to," he said, and then he left.

After he exited the room, Little Kevin sat back down on the bed next to his sister. "He scared you, huh?"

"Um, yeah, at first," she replied with uncertainty. "Did he scare you?"

"Nope," he said proudly.

"Think he's gonna bring us the McDonald's?"

"I don't know."

"Well, I hope he does, because I am *really* hungry."

"Don't worry, we'll be back home soon."

"You think so?" Kammy said, sounding worried.

"Of course, we are. Mommy and Daddy are looking for us as we speak."

"But what if they never find us?"

"Stop being negative. They will."

Kammy let out a long sigh. "I sure hope you're right," she said. Then she flopped down on the bed.

CHAPTER 9

Kevin

I DREADED GOING HOME, BECAUSE I KNEW AVA WAS GOING TO BE waiting, front and center, when I walked through the front door. I rehearsed over and over again what I was going to tell her when the conversation came up about Ty and my out-of-wedlock baby. I also knew that I wasn't going to be prepared for what she was going to say after I laid everything out on the table. Ava came with a lot of surprises, and she was very unpredictable. I just hoped I could get through the night and be one step closer to getting our kids back.

After I entered the house, I found Ava lying in bed, crying her eyes out, when I walked into the bedroom. My heart went out to her because I knew she was not only reeling from the fact that our kids were in the hands of unknown kidnappers, but she also had to deal with the affair I'd been having—and I brought another baby into the world. So I climbed on the bed and tried to put my arms around her. The moment I touched her, she unleashed fury my way.

"Get away from me, you fucking cheater!" she roared as she elbowed me in the chest.

Crippled by her outburst, I backed away from her and off the bed without saying a word; this infuriated her even more. She sat up on the bed and faced me head-on. Her face was drenched in tears. I could tell that she had been crying for hours.

"I can't believe that you had a fucking baby on me, Kevin," she started off.

I stood there alongside the bed, not knowing what to say. I figured if I said something, it would be the wrong thing, so I didn't say anything. And this didn't sit well with her.

"Did you not hear what I just said?" she snapped, and threw a pillow at me. I blocked it with my forearms, and it fell back on the bed.

"What do you want me to say?" I finally said.

"I wanna know why would you do this to me? I thought we were good. I thought what we had was enough."

Not knowing how to answer her question, I just stood there dumbfounded. My silence only escalated her level of rage.

"Don't just stand there looking stupid. Answer my question!" she shouted.

"What do you want me to say?" I replied.

"I want you to tell me what happened. When did you meet her? And when did you guys got serious enough to the point where you decided to have a baby, all while already having a fucking family here?" she bawled.

I thought for a moment about whether or not now would be the time to be brutally honest with Ava, and what effect it would have on her, considering everything going on right now dealing with the kids. I mean, I could lie and tell her Ty was a side chick that I didn't really care for, and my baby was a mistake, but then I figured things would only get worse when the real truth came out later. I would've liked to protect her feelings, but it was too late.

"Spill it, dammit!" she urged me.

"Look, Ava, it all happened so fast," I started off saying, while trying to gather the right words in my head.

"I don't wanna hear that shit. Tell me where you met her?"

Oh, my God, should I tell her the truth? I suddenly thought.

"Tell me, Kevin!" she shouted once again.

"She's a flight attendant," I finally admitted.

"So you met her while you were flying?"

"Yes."

"When?"

"About a year and a half ago." I lied. Didn't want Ava to really know how long Ty and I had been seeing one another.

"So, did y'all exchange numbers at that time?"

"Yes."

"So, who came on to whom?"

"She came on to me," I lied. I couldn't let on that I had pursued Ty.

"And you fell for it, huh?"

I refused to answer.

"What did she say to you?" Ava asked as she folded her arms and locked them. At one point it looked like she snarled at me.

"I don't exactly remember, Ava. It was so long ago," I lied once again. I really wanted to avoid rehashing any of the conversations I had with Ty when we first met. I'd be setting myself up for Ava to throw every word back at me when she got mad at me. No way.

"Did you get her number, or she got yours?"

"I don't know."

"Oh, you fucking know, Kevin! Tell the truth, you gave that bitch your number after she turned around and showed you her ass. She probably even sucked your dick in the bathroom."

"Ava, she didn't suck my dick."

"But I'm sure she's sucking it now!" she screamed.

"Come on now, Ava, is that necessary?" I said calmly.

"You are fucking right it's necessary! You fucked a bitch you met on a flight to God knows where and started a relationship with her. Then you got the bitch pregnant. Now, how fucked-up is that? I thought we had something good here. You promised me that you'd never cheat on me, and you did it. You're no different than fucking Nick. To be perfectly honest, you're fucking worse. At least when he cheated, he didn't bring a baby back," she pointed out.

You know what? She was right. Everything she said was spot-on. Yeah, Nick was a cheater, too, and I promised her that I wouldn't ever cheat on her. But I did and I brought a baby into the mix.

"I am so sorry, Ava," I apologized.

"Is that all you can say? *Sorry?*"

"What else do you want me to say?"

"I want you to undo all this bullshit."

"But I can't."

"Do you love her?"

I hesitated, refusing to answer that question, because I knew Ava wouldn't want to hear the truth.

"Answer me, goddammit!" she roared.

"Yes, yes, I do."

She swayed her head back and forth as if absorbed with pain and agony. "Damn, Kev, you could've at least lied to me. Do you know how gut-wrenching it felt to hear you tell me that you loved her? Do you know how that just made me feel? And especially with everything going on with our kids?" she expressed.

"I'm sorry, Ava. Really, I am."

"Yeah, I bet you are," she commented, and then she said, "So the little girl's name is Annabelle, huh?"

"How did you know?" I asked her. Then it quickly dawned on me that she had to have gotten that information from Nick. Besides my dad, he was the only other person who knew about my little girl.

"Cut it out, you know who told me," she replied sarcastically. "He couldn't wait to tell me. Told me where the bitch lived. When you had the fucking bastard baby and all. Y'all are just playing little house on the prairie out there in Richmond, huh? Me and the kids you had here weren't enough that you had to go out there and start another fucking family? Just think that if your black ass was here, our kids would've still been at home. But no! You had your ass laid up in another woman's bed, fucking her brains out, while a couple of bold motherfuckers decided they wanted to come in here and kidnap your other kids."

"So now you're trying to blame this on me?"

"You fucking right! Because if you were here then, no one would've dared to come in here and take our kids from us. But let's just say that they did, this whole thing is still your fault because they're asking for two million dollars. I don't have two million, but they think you do. So, whose fucking fault is it?"

"That's not fair, Ava."

"Get the fuck outta here, talking about it's not fair. You know what's not fair? You are bringing all this heartache on me, your family, and bringing bastard children into the world. And now I've gotta suffer because you can't keep your dick in your pants."

I stood there speechless.

"You're a piece of shit!"

I couldn't take any more of her verbal insults, so I turned around to leave the room and this sent her into a fury.

"Don't leave when I'm talking to you!" she screamed, and hopped off the bed.

Before I could get out of the bedroom door clean, Ava was down on my back, punching me as hard as she could. One blow hitting me after the other, up and down my spine. I whirled around and grabbed her into a bear hug. "Ava, stop it right now," I urged her, while trying to restrain her.

She got extremely wild after I added pressure to my grip around her. She started acting hysterically.

"Get off of me!" her voice boomed as she moved violently, trying to break free of my hold.

But I held on to her for dear life. "Calm down and I will let you go," I assured her.

"No, you're gonna let me go now," she hissed. I could see the venom slithering from her mouth.

There was one thing I knew about Ava—and that was when she was mad, and this was one of those times, there's no telling what she was capable of doing. It had gotten to a point where I knew that if she had a gun in her hand, she would've used it on me. Right then and there, I knew I had to let her go and do it in a way where she wouldn't retaliate against me, so I did.

Slowly I released her from my grip and talked to her calmly as I did so. "I'm letting you go, Ava, so don't do anything crazy," I said as I watched her closely. I also saw Paulina come up from behind me through my peripheral vision. I was glad that she came to see what was going on. Sometimes when she's in our presence, she has a way of calming Ava down. I waited for her to chime in at any given moment.

Ava eyed me evilly. "Fuck you!" she scoffed at me, and lunged a blow in my direction after turning around to face me.

"Wait, no, Mrs. Frost!" Paulina said, alerting me.

I couldn't get out of the way, but I dodged the blow with my arms. Ava tried to throw a few more punches at me, but I jumped backward and hightailed it out of the bedroom before she could get within arm's reach of me again.

"You motherfucker! Get out of my house!" Ava screeched.

I could hear the heat vibrations spewing out of her mouth and bouncing off the bedroom walls. I left Paulina in the room to deal with her tantrum. I knew there was nothing I could do at this point to defuse the situation.

CHAPTER 10

Ava

"P AULINA, I WANT HIM OUT OF HERE," I RETORTED AFTER I SPUN around, then faced her.

"Mrs. Frost, you're trembling," Paulina pointed out as she tried to console me.

"Paulina, he's gotta go!" I shouted as my verbal outburst turned into cries. "I want him out of my house." I began to sob again.

"Come on, Mrs. Frost, let me get you back in bed," she said, leading me back to my bed and helping me climb into it.

My tears started falling uncontrollably. I was an emotional mess. I also felt lost, especially now with my kids being gone. "Will you please lie down with me?" I asked Paulina.

"Sure," she said.

After Paulina climbed onto the bed next to me, she cradled me into her arms, like she always did when I was feeling down and needed to be held. This was her way of letting me know that everything would be all right.

"I appreciate you so much," I whispered; my words strained under the oxygen cannula in my nose.

"I know you do," she replied, and kissed me on my forehead.

I hadn't realized it at first that I had cried myself to sleep until I had awakened a few hours later. It was 2:35 A.M. and I was lying in bed alone. Paulina must've slipped out of my bed after I had fallen asleep. I also noticed that she had turned off my television, so it was quiet. When I thought about it, it was an eerie quietness. It wasn't normal. In fact, the tone enveloped my bedroom, and it whizzed its way through my entire home.

Curious to know where Kevin was, I climbed out of my bed and exited the bedroom. I searched every room in the house, and when I realized that he was nowhere in the house, I looked out my living-room window. His car wasn't there, either, so I knew then he had left the house altogether. I was instantly lit with fury. "That motherfucker really left me here," I grumbled, even though I knew I had ordered him to leave the house. In my mind he was supposed to stay here, regardless of what I told him. Men are supposed to stand up and be seen. Take charge. Not run away at the first sign of trouble. Fucking son of a bitch! It wouldn't surprise me if that bastard drove back up to Richmond to lay up with his mistress. I wished I knew where the bitch lived, because I would drive there in a fucking heartbeat and confront both of their asses. Knowing me, I'd probably beat her ass and drop his baby on her head and say "oops" after that. Boy, would that be gratifying.

After pacing the floors in my house for twenty minutes, I retired back to my bedroom and climbed back into bed. I tried to go back to sleep, but I couldn't. I couldn't get my mind off that bastard I was married to—and my children. Thinking about my kids really hit a low for me. I couldn't stop imagining, what if they were being hurt? I swear to God, if those motherfuckers inflicted any pain on my babies, I was going to make sure that they paid. I would make sure that it was done slowly. Nick would make sure of that. There's no question in my mind. He was a thoroughbred type of guy. Tough guy in every sense. Well-known in the streets and with a ton of respect.

I knew for a fact that if I had married him and we shared kids, this would not have happened. No one in their right mind would dare kidnap Nick's kids. That's just how much he was feared. But the idiot I was married to was a joke. No one feared him. Not even his children, and that's why they ran over top of him. But no, I had to fall for his good-guy persona, and look where that got me! Missing children, a mistress, and a bastard baby. How fucked-up is that? But it's all good because I would bounce back. After I got my children back and made this huge financial lick, I was leaving that piece-of-shit husband of mine and I would be out of here permanently. If Paulina wanted to come with me, she could. If not, I was gone and I was not looking back.

While mulling over my escape plan, I felt the urge to call Nick's cell phone. I knew he would answer it, because he never really slept. I've known him for over fifteen years, and I've only seen him sleep for no more than four hours a day, and that could be any time of the day. "Hello," he greeted me after he answered my FaceTime call. He smiled, giving off his handsome-ass smile.

I had to admit that he was fine as hell. But he's a cheater at heart, so he couldn't be trusted. "Hello to you, too," I greeted him. "You still at the garage?"

"No, I'm home now. Whatcha doing up this late?" he wanted to know.

"You know I can't sleep when my babies aren't here."

"I'm sure. But where is Kevin?"

"I'm not sure. I dozed off earlier, and when I got up a few minutes ago, he wasn't here."

"You know he called me back after you left my office today."

"What did he say?"

"He wanted to know if you had agreed to do the job for me."

"What did you say?"

"I told him that it wasn't my place to say and that he needed to speak with you. Did he question you about it?"

"No, he didn't mention it. But I got in his shit about that ho he fucked and had a baby with."

"So he didn't deny it?"

"How could he? He literally took a picture with the baby and the bitch."

Nick chuckled. "Besides that, how are you dealing with the situation with your kids?"

"It's so hard, Nick. I think about them constantly, all day. Wondering if the people who have them are mistreating or hurting them. It would break my heart if they're being hurt in any way."

"Listen, if this helps any, I've put the word out on the streets that whoever has them better not hurt them—or I will find out who they are, and I will deal with them personally."

"You did that for me?" I questioned him with a lighter heart. His gesture definitely made me feel just a little bit better.

"Of course, I did. I made some calls right after you left today. I even took it a little further and put a tracker out there to see if someone knew who was behind it."

"You think you'd be able to get them back without paying the ransom?" I asked optimistically.

"Now, I don't know about that. But I'm sure I can find out who's behind it and make sure that they're taking good care of your kids."

"Nick, I sure appreciate that. I just wished that Kevin had respect like you."

"See, if you would've stuck it out with me, you wouldn't be going through this shit," Nick chastised me. It was more like an *I told you so* spiel. I started to remind him of the times he cheated on me, too, but I didn't feel like dredging up old shit. Besides,

Nick and I hadn't been together in years and we're in a good place, so I prefer to stay there.

"You know it's so crazy you said that, because I was thinking that same thing earlier," I admitted.

"You know, we would've been good together," he insisted.

I didn't want to hear that shit. Nick was full of shit. He's *never* been a one-woman man. He has to have multiple women, and that won't work for me. I'm shocked that he doesn't have any children, especially with all of the women he's fucked.

"You think so?" I answered. That was the only rebuttal I could think of.

"Of course."

"Let me ask you something."

"What's up?"

"Why haven't you ever had any children?"

"That's a good question. I don't know. I guess no one wants to have a baby by me," he said jokingly, cracking a smile.

"You sure you don't have any babies out there you don't know about?"

"Trust me, if I did, I'd know about it."

I sighed heavily, thinking about the baby Kevin just had. "I can't believe Kevin went outside of our marriage and had a baby on me."

"Well, believe it, because it happened. Now, what are you going to do about it?"

"What can I do? The damage is done."

"Are you sticking around?"

"You mean, am I getting a divorce?"

"Yeah."

"Oh, I'm definitely leaving that son of a bitch!"

"Coming back home to me?" Nick asked jokingly. It was one of those questions where he asked in a joking way, but I knew that he was serious.

"No, Nick, I am not," I replied with utmost sincerity. I couldn't give him the slightest indication there was a chance he and I could get back together. My days with Nick were long gone. He hurt me once and I would never let him do it again.

"Ah, come on now, Ava. You know I would treat you good."

"But remember, you cheated on me, too."

"Look how long ago that was. I was young and stupid. Didn't know what I had. I would never put you through that ever again. You're the love of my life. Do you know that I've never loved another woman the way I loved you?"

"No, I didn't know that," I said nonchalantly. Because in all honesty I really didn't care. Nick is a womanizer, and he doesn't love anyone but himself. It's just as simple as that.

"Well, it's true. No one will ever be able to fill this spot, right here in my heart," he acknowledged as he pointed to his chest.

I've got to admit that I wasn't fazed by his *Romeo and Juliet* bullshit! Nick was who Nick was—a bullshit artist—and I wasn't falling for his shit.

I changed the subject. I was not gonna sit here and listen to his lies. I was already dealing with one cheating asshole; I was not about to go backward and deal with an old one. "So let me ask you, what time do you want me to come by and start my day off?" I asked.

"Come by at the top of the morning. That way I can get you photographed to get you your ID to get on the terminal and then we can go over last-minute plans."

"Okay. Sounds good."

"Are you nervous?"

I let out a long sigh. "No, I just wanna get this over with so we can get this money and I can get my babies back."

Nick smiled at me. "Enough said."

CHAPTER 11

Kevin

HEARING MY CELL PHONE RING SCARED ME OUT OF MY SLEEP. After I opened my eyes, I realized I had left it on the nightstand next to the bed and grabbed it. By this time it had rung three times.

"Hello," I answered.

"Hey, baby, you up?" Ty asked. I could hear my baby girl in the background crying.

"I'm up now. What's wrong with her?" I asked.

"I don't know. She's been fussing all morning. I bathed her, gave her a bottle, and she's still cranky about something."

"Maybe her stomach hurts," I suggested.

"Yeah, I thought about that."

"She could have colic, too. Have you checked her temperature?"

"Yeah, I did. It was 98.2, so she's fine," Ty replied.

"Well, if she keeps crying, call her doctor."

"I will," she assured me. "So, how did you sleep last night? I couldn't believe it when you called and told me that you were going to a hotel."

"Yeah, I had to get out of that house last night before something happened that I would've regretted later."

"Has she tried to call you?" Ty asked.

"Nope."

"Have you tried to call her?"

"Nope."

"So, are you going back to the house when you check out?"

"Yeah, I'm gonna go back and see if Ava or my nanny has heard from the kidnappers. Then I'm gonna take a shower and change clothes so I can go back to the office."

"Have you talked to the kidnappers since they took your kids?"

"Nope."

"And that doesn't concern you?"

"It kinda does. But they gave us specific instructions and told us that we had seventy-two hours to come up with the money. So, I guess, we'll hear from them then."

"Are you close to getting it?" Ty wanted to know.

I sighed once again. "Not quite, but I will be, soon enough."

"But what if you don't come up with it?"

"I have no other choice."

"But what if you don't?"

"What's up with you?" I snapped. "Why you being so negative?"

"I'm just asking a question. Don't be such an asshole about it!" she tossed back. I could still hear our baby crying in the background. It was beginning to annoy me.

"Look, why don't you concentrate on calming her down and call me back later," I said to Ty.

"But I'm not done talking." She sounded disappointed.

"What else is there to say?" I asked her. At this point I wanted to end the call and concentrate on how I was going to come up with this money to get my kids back. Listening to her nag me about nonsense wasn't doing it.

"Does she want a divorce?" Ty came out of the blue and asked me.

"She hasn't said it," I told her nonchalantly.

"Do you want one?" She was pressing me.

"Look, Ty, I don't wanna talk about that right now."

"Why are you avoiding it? You already said it was a matter of time before y'all get a divorce. Now that she knows about me and the baby, this is the perfect setup."

"Look, I'm not about to do this now. I'll call you later," I said. Then I abruptly disconnected our call. I sat there and waited for her to call me back, but after waiting for five minutes, I realized that she wasn't going to, so I was relieved. Going back and forth with her wasn't what I wanted, especially not in the mind frame I was in. For my peace of mind, I decided to deal with her bullshit later.

CHAPTER 12

Ty

"H ELLO! HELLO!" I SAID, JUST REALIZING THIS NEGRO HAD hung up on me. How dare he? After all the shit I have put up with, he wants to hang up on me. Shit, *I'm* the good woman. *I'm* the perfect one. *I'm* in better shape, am more fit and educated than her.

From what I'm told by Kevin, she served time in prison for being involved in a car theft ring. So she's a freaking criminal— a hood rat—and judging from the way Kevin talks about her, she's even a nag. Besides that, I've seen her Instagram page. I can't believe how she parades around on social media, like her life is perfect. Doing TikTok videos with the kids, like their life is so wonderful. But the whole time her husband, and their daddy, is over here playing house with me and Annabelle. Too bad for them. I know this may sound harsh, but it wouldn't be such a bad thing if they never get their kids back. Kevin needs to be here in Richmond with me and Annabelle anyway. The other kids are just in the way of us having him all to ourselves. He just doesn't know it, but he will be better off with us and not them.

* * *

I finally got Annabelle to settle down. I can't tell you why she was cranky earlier, I'm just glad the crying stopped. I tried to get Kevin back on the phone, but he didn't answer. I assumed that maybe he had gone home and was having a major powwow with Ava, so I figured he'd call me back when he got the chance. I can't lie, it bothered me that I couldn't talk to him whenever I wanted. I was the mother of his child—I should be able to have access to him all the time. But in this situation I didn't. I guess that's what happens when you're the other woman. You have to live by side-chick rules. The wife always comes first, and the mistress always comes second. You can only talk to him at certain times of the day. He can't spend every night with you, and God forbid if he has kids, you've got to share your time with them as well. It's a hot damn mess. I was warned by my family and my homegirl not to get deeply involved with Kevin, since I would have to share him with his wife and other kids, but I didn't listen. I fell for his charm and was sucked in by his generosity. Oh, my God! This guy showered me with all sorts of expensive gifts. I have everything from a Rolex watch, to Tiffany bracelets, designer handbags, designer shoes, and a big-ass diamond engagement ring, even though he hasn't officially asked me to marry him. I think it was more like a push present that cost $50,000. Besides that, he even upgraded my old 2018 Honda Accord to a brand-new Tesla. Now, how can I say no to all of that?

I believe this guy was made for me. We are meant to be soulmates. It will be revealed to him sooner than he thinks. I can guarantee you that. We will live happily ever after.

CHAPTER 13

Ava

O N MY WAY OUT OF THE HOUSE, I FORWARDED ALL THE HOUSE calls to my cell phone, just in case the kidnappers decided they wanted to call. I even gave Paulina instructions on what needed to be done while I was gone. She noted everything and I made my exit.

In the car I got a call from my dad. He decided to check on me this morning, since he didn't get a chance to make it back over to my house last night, due to the fact that my mother's nurse had to leave early. We chatted for a bit while on the route to Nick's garage.

"Sorry, I couldn't make it back over there last night," he started off.

"Dad, no need for apologies. I told you that last night."

"How are you feeling this morning?"

"I'm feeling a ton of anxiety because I've got until Saturday to come up with all of the money."

"Where is Kevin?"

"Not sure."

"What do you mean you're not sure? He's supposed to be right by your side through all of this."

74

"Dad, Kevin is having an affair," I confessed. My heart was thundering in my chest. I was tired of holding this secret in and acting like everything was perfect. My kids were missing, and I needed to get them back. Plus, my husband had started another family on me. My father needed to know what was really going on in his daughter's life.

"He's *what?*" my father roared through the phone line. I knew his blood was boiling now.

"I saw a photo of him, the woman, and a brand-new baby. I found it in his luggage right after you left the house yesterday. I found out the woman lives in Richmond, and they've been seeing each other for over a year and a half, I'm told," I continued telling him.

"That piece of shit!" he growled. "How could he do that to you and the kids?"

"That's what I said when I found out."

"And what did he say?"

"He couldn't say anything. The damage is already done."

"So, how old is that baby?"

"A couple of months, I think."

"Boy or girl?"

"Girl."

"I wanna rip him a new asshole," my father huffed. I could hear the anger inside of him building intensely.

"Calm down, Dad, I'm gonna handle him right after I get my babies back."

"You know what, I'm calling that son of a bitch right now. I'll call you back," he continued, and before I could reply, he ended our call.

CHAPTER 14

Kevin

I HADN'T BEEN OUT OF THE SHOWER TEN MINUTES BEFORE MY CELL phone started blowing up. When I looked at the phone screen and saw that it was Ava's father, I honestly had no idea what kind of conversation we were going to have. See, Ava's father is a bull-headed, stubborn old man. Ava mentioned to me that when she was growing up, her dad was a hardnose, and he ran their household like a military camp. I'm sure it had a lot to do with the fact that he served in the Gulf War. But according to Ava, he ruled with an iron fist and her mother never intervened in the way he disciplined Ava.

As Ava got older, she grew tired of her father's strict house rules and left home when she was just seventeen years old. Not too long after, she met Nick and that's when she got into the life of stealing cars. Her father was outraged and cut her off for a bit. They reestablished their relationship sometime later and he's been safeguarding her ever since.

"Hey, Arthur, what's up?"

"Don't 'Hey, Arthur' me, you son of a bitch! What is this I hear? You're having an affair on Ava and had a freaking baby!

Then to make matters worse, you pull this shit during the worst fucking time," he grumbled.

I wasn't at all shocked by his question. I knew that I would be confronted by him, sooner or later. I dared not disrespect Arthur, either, for the sake of my wife, so I took a deep breath and then I exhaled.

"Why don't you stop by the house later and we'll talk about it," I finally said.

"No, you're gonna tell me why you went out and cheated on my baby girl and then had a fucking baby on her?" His tone echoed through the phone and into my ear.

"No disrespect, sir, but I can't talk about that right now. I've got to stay focused on getting my kids back," I said calmly, hoping he'd back down and give me a break, being that I mentioned his grandkids.

"Now, see, that's the other thing, you're 'round here cheating on my daughter, bringing another baby into this world, while a couple of thugs kidnapped my grandchildren out of their beds."

"Arthur, you don't think that is tearing my soul apart?" I yelled. He had hit a nerve, blaming me for my children's kidnapping because of my absence. How fucking dare he! It's bad enough that I have to deal with the fact that I don't know where they're at or who has them, but I can't carry that burden, too.

"Cheating on your wife should be tearing up your soul! Ava is a good woman. She gave you two beautiful children, and she takes good damn care of them, too. She even provides a clean and stable environment for those kids, so how could you fuck that up for a piece of ass?"

"Arthur, I told you I don't wanna discuss that with you right now."

"Oh, we're gonna discuss it, whether you like it or not," he demanded.

I wasn't going to let that old man bully me. Not now, not ever.

"Hey, Arthur, I'm sorry, but I'm gonna have to take this call," I lied. Then I abruptly disconnected the call before he could utter another word.

Immediately after I pressed the END button, I tossed my cell phone on the bed that Ava and I shared and then I proceeded to get dressed. A couple of minutes later, my phone rang again. I reached back, picked it up, and noticed it was Arthur calling me back. I wasn't about to answer his call, so I tossed my phone right back on my bed. It rang several more times and then it stopped. I guess he got the message, because I've got other shit to do besides sit on the phone with him and let him talk shit to me about me cheating on Ava. Okay, yeah, I knew I fucked up. But what can I do about it now? Nothing. What I am going to do is concentrate on getting this money so I can get my kids back. Simple as that.

After I had gotten dressed, I headed into my kids' bedrooms to look around, hoping to find some type of clue as to who had come into my house and kidnapped them. When I couldn't find anything, I went downstairs to take a look at all the doors that led outside, to see if they were broken into. When I realized the locks on the doors weren't tampered with, this instantly struck me as an inside job, so I called out to Paulina, who was in the kitchen rearranging things. I asked her to come to the living room. She joined me a few minutes later.

"Who found the ransom note? You or Ava?" I got straight to the point.

"Mrs. Ava found it," Paulina responded.

"And where were you?"

"I was in my bedroom when she called my name. I rushed out and that's when she told me that she couldn't find the kids."

"And what did you do when she told you that?" I wanted to know. I watched her body language closely.

"I searched both of the kids' rooms, their closets, and everywhere I thought they might be hiding," she explained.

"And didn't hear anything at all that night or early morning?"

"No, not a thing."

"See, I don't believe that, because I just looked at all the doors and it doesn't seem like the house was broken into. It looked like it was an inside job."

"What are you saying?" Paulina asked.

"What I'm saying is, did you have something to do with my kids getting kidnapped?" I confronted her.

Shocked and somewhat puzzled, Paulina flopped down on the chair that was right next to her, reacting as if she'd been gut punched. "I don't know what you're implying," she said.

"Just tell me the truth. Tell me what happened!" I pressured her.

"What do you mean, tell you the truth? There's nothing to tell," she said, giving off an expression of confusion.

"Paulina, don't bullshit me now! Just tell me the truth. Did you let the fucking kidnappers into my home?" I roared at her. I could feel my nostrils flaring up.

"I didn't do anything wrong, Mr. Frost. You know I love those kids. I treat them like they're my grandchildren," she tried to explain as she began to sob. She was getting upset very quickly.

"Cut the shit, Paulina! Because there's no way that those motherfuckers got into my house without any help! Ava wouldn't have let them in, so you had to do it," I shouted, shooting venom out of my mouth.

Visibly shaken, Paulina held out her hands and cried out, "I didn't let anyone in this house!"

"Then tell me why you didn't hear the intruders when they entered my home?" I wouldn't let up. I interrogated her like a cop would do a murder suspect. My kids' lives were at stake, and I needed answers.

But then, without saying another word, Paulina reached down

into her pants pocket and retrieved her cell phone. After she activated the phone keypad, I knew she was about to call Ava. So I stood there and waited for what was to come next, because I wasn't about to back down.

"Mrs. Frost," she started off saying, her voice trembling while she sobbed quietly.

I thought I heard Ava ask in an alarmed fashion, "What is it, Paulina?"

"Mr. Frost thinks that I let the kidnappers in the house." She broke down crying uncontrollably.

In a flash Ava started screaming through the phone, but I couldn't clearly hear what she was saying; her words were barely audible. Judging from Paulina's face, I knew Ava was talking shit about me, because the nanny's demeanor was becoming calmer by the second. Seeing this unfold before my eyes started ruffling my feathers.

"What is she saying to you?" I demanded to know.

She ignored me and continued to listen to what Ava was telling her. I snatched her cell phone from her hand and put the call on speakerphone. Ava was spewing out venom.

"Don't listen to any of that shit he's talking. I know you didn't have anything to do with what happened to my babies—"

"And how do you know that for sure? You were asleep!" I shouted back. I was furious.

"And your cheating ass was with your mistress playing house! So, what the hell are you saying?" she yelled out even louder. "And how dare you accuse Paulina of doing something like that? She loves those kids," she added.

"You've watched Lifetime movies before, housekeepers and nannies get kids kidnapped all the fucking time," I blasted her. At this point I was shooting down everything she was throwing at me. I wanted to get down to where my kids were, and if Paulina knew more than what she was letting on.

"Kevin, leave Paulina alone, right now! You hear me? I will deal with you when I get home!" Ava screamed, and then she ended the call abruptly.

Paulina stood up from the chair, snatched her cell phone from my hand, and then she stormed off.

"Don't think just because you called Ava, I'm going to leave you alone. I'm gonna find out if you let those motherfuckers in my house!" I shouted at the top of my voice.

I heard Paulina head up to her bedroom and close the door behind her. I had no other reason to be here at the house, so I grabbed my keys and headed for the front door. I figured I couldn't get anything done here. None of my money was here, nor was the Rolodex of phone numbers I needed to contact those who owed me money, so it was time to go.

CHAPTER 15

Ava

I WAS ESCORTED INTO NICK'S WAREHOUSE BY ONE OF HIS MECHANICS and then into his back office. When he saw me walk in, I found him sitting behind his desk, sifting through paperwork that was scattered across his desk. His eyes were locked on a set of blueprints, but then he looked up at me and gave me the biggest smile ever. I smiled back and walked toward his desk. From what I could tell, the blueprints were that of a house—a big one at that.

"Building a new house?" I inquired after leaning in over his desk.

"Yes, I am," he said boldly. "It's going to be eight thousand square feet, on ten acres of land," he added.

I looked down at the architectural drawings and saw a triple set of gables that would accent the front entrance. Then I saw a two-story foyer that would make the grand entrance. Spacious windows would give expansive views all around the home. Not to mention, the design for the gourmet kitchen was far more impressive than anyone could imagine—with a large central island and cooktop, walk-in pantry, and an area for the dining table spacious enough for a party of ten. Even the design for the bedrooms was spectacular. I couldn't get over the fact that the master suite view of the courtyard was within eye's reach. And the patio would be encased with elegant iron bars.

"Who are you building this home for?" I asked him point-blank.

"I would've been building it for you. But you had to run off and marry my best friend," he said jokingly. But I knew he was serious. I shrugged off his comment and continued to admire the rest of the design.

Meanwhile, my cell phone rang, and I noticed it was Kevin calling, but I refused to answer. I pressed the END button, and what do you know? He called me right back. So I ended the call again. And he called me back a third time.

"Maybe you ought to answer that," Nick suggested.

"It's Kevin calling me back and I don't want to talk to him right now."

"Maybe it's about the kids? Or maybe he got the money?" Nick commented.

A light in my head went off, because for a moment I believed that Nick could be right. But by the time I answered the phone, it had stopped ringing. I immediately called Kevin back. He answered on the second ring.

"Hello," he said.

"You called?" I replied.

"I forgot to tell you when we were on the phone earlier that I got a call from your father," he said irritably.

"And?" I responded sarcastically, because in my head I knew where this was going.

"Why did you have to go and tell him what's going on between us?" he yelled.

"Are you fucking kidding me right now? You have the nerve to call and ask me why I told my father that you fucked around on me and had a baby with some other bitch?" I shouted. I mean, was this guy really serious now?

The tone of his voice decreased right away. "I thought that we kept our personal business in the house."

"Did you keep your dick in the house?" I continued to shout. By this point I had become livid. I mean, how dare this bastard call me and question me about what I discuss with my father, especially after he violated and defiled our marriage by sleeping with another woman? Was he out of his fucking mind? I mean, was I wrong for telling my father that the man I loved, married, and had children with, and was supposed to honor and protect me, broke a sacred bond? Who the hell else was I supposed to tell? My mother? She's going through dementia, and I don't have any siblings.

So, what did he expect from me? A code of secrecy? Everything we said at the altar went out the window as soon as he fucked the next chick. Now all bets were off.

"Look, if you didn't call to tell me that you got the rest of the money to get our kids back, I have nothing else to say to you," I continued.

"I'm still working on that."

"Well, I'll tell you what. Don't call me back until you get the rest of the money," I said.

Kevin then changed the subject on me. "Where are you?"

"Why?"

"Because I wanna know. Don't want anything happening to you, too," he claimed.

"Don't worry about me, I'll be fine," I told him. Then I ended the call.

After I pushed my cell phone back down into my pocket, I realized Nick was staring at me. I shook my head, giving off the impression that I was disgusted by the mere fact that Kevin had the balls to call and question me, considering his indiscretions.

"You all right?" Nick asked.

"I will be, after I get this money and get my babies back."

"So I take it he doesn't have the money?"

"Nah, he's more concerned about me telling my father that he fucked around on me than trying to get up the money to pay our kids' ransom."

"That's messed up," Nick said.

"Tell me about it," I agreed while shaking my head.

Nick continued to look over the blueprints of his new home until I brought up the subject of the car heist we were supposed to pull off. I got straight to the point. I'm the type of person who doesn't like to wait until the last minute to put a plan together. I like to be prepared for jobs I do, especially the ones of this magnitude.

"So, what's the plan?" I asked.

"Well, we won't have access to the actual keys, so I've got this guy who's gonna bring by a handheld device that has a software installed in it that will allow you to open the car door and start the ignition without the actual key fob."

"When is he bringing it by?"

"He should be here any moment."

"How much is that gonna run you?"

"The device alone is running me two hundred grand. The code for each car is costing me fifty thousand a pop," Nick revealed.

"That's a nice piece of change. I sure hope they work," I remarked.

"Oh, they will. Trust me."

"Do you have a picture of the container it's coming in?" I wanted to know.

"As a matter of fact, I do," he assured me, pulling photos out from his desk drawer.

I looked over the photos closely. The color of the container was gray. A popular color for most of the containers on a shipping terminal. What stuck out to me was the lettering on the side. It read: OPLG. OPLG was a company that shipped high-end foreign goods. The only people who knew it were wealthy people who used that shipping service. Ordinary people weren't aware of this company. But Nick and I were.

"Are there any more of these OPLG containers coming into the port tonight?" I asked.

"There's one more, but it contains some paintings."

"Is the container the same color?"

"No, it's red," Nick answered.

"Okay, good."

"What about the GPS sensor deactivator?" I inquired.

"Don't worry, I have one right here for you," he assured me while pulling one out from the same drawer he had pulled the photos from.

"Okay, good," I responded. "What section of the terminal will this container be in?"

Nick pulled out a map of the terminal and pointed to the location; then he showed me where I had to drive the car, once I got possession of it.

"Who's gonna be my driver?"

"You'll be jumping in the truck with Hank. He's going to get you on the terminal. And he's gonna drop you off near the container. After you've driven the car into the designated container, he will pick you back up at this point." Nick pointed to the pickup point on the map, indicating how far I had to walk to get back to Hank's truck. Judging from the distance, I thought it was only three hundred yards of walking distance. I could jog and get to him in less than two minutes.

"How do you feel?"

I took in a deep breath and then I exhaled. "I feel good."

"Think you can pull this off?"

"Of course, I can," I stated confidently.

"All right, well, let's do it," he said cheerfully.

I stood there looking down at the plans Nick had displayed before me, picturing myself on the terminal pulling off this job. I remember back in my heyday when I used to boost cars, it was nothing for me to lift ten cars in a day. I'm talking exotic cars and I used to get top dollar for them, too. If I stole a car worth $100,000, I took it to Nick, and he sold it for $60,000. I got my cut—thirty grand—and he pocketed the other thirty grand. It was that simple. So to see that I was about to come up on almost $10,00,000 is a whole other level. I will admit this is a tricky job. Actually, it's more of a risk, but when I think about my babies, I would steal those cars over and over again, if given the opportunity to do so.

While I was in deep thought, an unexpected guest popped her head in Nick's office. "Hey there, handsome," I heard the familiar voice say. I didn't have to look up to see the familiar voice belonged to Lacey, who was Nick's older sister. She was a bitch, too. She hated my guts because I left Nick and started dating, and eventually married, Kevin. Every so often she'll remind me of how fucked I was for fucking two best friends. I figured today might not be any different.

Nick smiled, walked over to the door of his office, and hugged Lacey. "What brings you here?"

"Maceo has some business with this guy in Virginia Beach. So we flew out here for a day. We're leaving on the last flight out of here tonight, though," she explained.

"Why are you leaving so soon?" Nick wanted to know.

"Because we've gotta get back to what we got going on back west," she added.

"That's understandable," Nick said as he nodded his head.

Lacey immediately turned her attention toward me. "Surprised to see you here," she didn't hesitate to say.

"I was actually invited here by your brother," I told her.

"Oh, really? Wonder why?" she said as she turned her attention toward Nick.

"Come on now, Lacey, let's be nice," Nick commented.

"I'm being nice." Lacey smiled mischievously as she moved toward me.

"Sounds like sarcasm to me," I made it a point to say.

"Oh, you haven't seen sarcasm yet," Lacey insisted.

"Lacey, not now. Please," Nick begged her. He knew she was confrontational, and the fact that she didn't like me, there was an argument on the horizon.

"All I wanna do is ask her how she could show her face back around here after running off, fucking your best friend, and then marrying him?"

"That's none of your damn business!" I shot her an evil stare.

"Oh, but it is my business."

Nick stood there, shaking his head in despair.

"And how is that?" I questioned her.

"Because that's my brother and he is my business," she answered.

"Why don't you ask him why I ran off with his best friend, since you're so concerned."

"I wanna hear it from you. You're the one who did the running off."

"Lacey, please let it go," Nick pleaded with her.

"No, she needs to take accountability for her actions. I mean, she did fuck your best friend, and then having kids with him was a major slap in the face, especially after all the shit you did for her ass."

"Especially after all the shit he did for me! I beg your pardon, Lacey!" I roared. She had definitely hit a nerve. "Let me remind you that I worked my ass off for your brother when we were together, so everything I got, I earned. I was your brother's best booster and I made him millions," I added.

"Yeah, and you also bailed on him after the cops locked him up," she replied sarcastically.

"After I found out that he was fucking around on me," I snapped, and then I turned my attention toward Nick. "Did you tell her that the bitch you were fucking called my phone and told me that she was pregnant before you made her get an abortion and that you guys had been together for six months?" I asked him, my heart rate began to pick up. This sister of his was getting me amped up.

"I don't care what he says, you don't just go off and fuck his best friend. That's ho behavior."

"Bitch, I am not a ho!" I boomed. My blood pressure had shot through the roof. Yep, Lacey had definitely gotten me to my breaking point.

"All right, enough, Lacey," Nick spoke up.

"No, it's all right, let her talk. I'm gonna go," I insisted.

"I'll call you later then," Nick told me.

"You do that," I replied right before exiting the office.

As soon as I got into my car, I took a deep breath and then I exhaled. The heated argument I had just had with Nick's sister was definitely unexpected and couldn't have come at a worse time. I mean, I wasn't in the mood to argue with her about why I left Nick. I wasn't there for that. I was there to talk about a job that would bring me the money I needed to get my kids back. But no, this bitch wants to show up and defend her fucking brother, who caused our breakup. Never mind who it was I decided to be with after the fact, because that's none of their business. Besides, it's been over ten years since Nick and I broke up. And by that alone, I could tell that she'd been waiting a long time to give me a piece of her mind. What a waste of time and energy. Stupid bitch!

CHAPTER 16

Nick

T O SEE LACEY ATTACK AVA THE WAY SHE DID WAS SOMEWHAT BITTER-
sweet. While Ava deserved every unkind word my sister hurled
at her, there was a time and a place for it. Today was definitely
not it. Okay, granted, Ava committed the ultimate betrayal, and
it sounded better hearing Lacey call her out on her shit, but Ava
and I were conducting business now, so I wish she would've
waited to do it another time.

"You see she got her ass out of here?" Lacey pointed out. She
was not pleased with Ava's presence.

I let out a long sigh. "Yeah" was all I could say.

"What was she doing here anyway?" Lacey questioned me.

"I'm thinking about bringing her in on the job," I told her,
even though I had already made up my mind. I brought it to my
sister in this manner to feel her out.

"The one Maceo and I put you on?" She wanted clarity.

"Yeah."

"No way, Nick. She doesn't deserve to get in on that one."

"Lacey, I couldn't agree with you more. But she's the only one
who can pull it off."

"You can't get any one of your other guys to do it?"

90

"I can only think of one, but I can't trust that he'll bring it back without a scratch on it. See, Ava is a precision driver. She's fast and skillful behind the wheel. There's no doubt in my mind that she'll get both of those cars and deliver them to their designated storage containers without any hiccups. Come on now, you know she's a pro at this," I tried convincing Lacey.

"What's her cut?"

"She and I haven't discussed it yet," I lied.

"I wouldn't give her shit, if you wanna know what I think. Besides, doesn't her husband owe you a shitload of cash?" Lacey asked.

"Yeah, he does, and that's one of the reasons I want to bring her in on this," I explained to Lacey. "Not only will she get the job done without any hiccups, I'll be able to kill two birds with one stone," I added.

"Does she know how much money he owes you?"

"Nope. We've never discussed it."

"Well, she should. Kevin wouldn't have been able to get all the shit he has if it wasn't for you."

"I know. But it's okay. Don't get all worked up. I am going to get all my money back. Believe me."

"You still love her, don't you?"

I started to answer my sister's question, but smiled bashfully instead.

She immediately became irritated. "For God's sake, Nick, she left you for your best friend."

"As much as I wanna choke her out every time I see her, I just keep reminding myself that I'll get my chance," I confessed.

"You should do it with this heist," Lacey said, her words sounding more like whispers as she walked closer to me. "Don't pay her shit after she does the jobs. I mean, what is she going to do? Call the Feds? Tell 'em she stole the cars and parked them into a container that's already on a ship sailing across the sea?"

"She might!" I joked.

"She wouldn't dare. Because if she did, she's going down all by her lonesome self. Not you or anyone else, for that matter. Speaking of which, does she know this job came from me and Maceo?"

"No, she doesn't know that you're involved."

"Good. Keep it that way. But I still say, stiff her at the end. She doesn't deserve to get a penny when it's all said and done." Lacey wouldn't let up.

She made it very clear that she didn't want Ava to make any money off this deal. As much as I agreed with her, I wasn't going to use her and then hang her out to dry.

I planned to pay her generously. But it wouldn't be what the going rate was.

CHAPTER 17

Ava

W HEN I ARRIVED HOME, PAULINA WAS WATCHING TELEVISION IN her room. I could tell that she was still visibly upset. I sat on the bed next to her and asked if she was okay, even though I knew that she wasn't.

"I won't feel better until my little ones are back, safe and sound," she said.

"They will be, don't worry," I assured her—even though I had doubted a few times if I'd ever see my babies again.

"Can you believe that Mr. Frost thinks I let the kidnappers into the house while you were asleep?"

"Who cares what he thinks? He's just looking for someone to blame. Take the heat off him and the affair he's been having with that skank."

"Well, he might be looking for someone to blame, but it still bothers me. Nevertheless, I'm not that kind of person, so I don't want to be looked at like that."

"Don't worry about him. His opinion doesn't matter. I know what happened. Besides that, I know what type of person you are. You're a good woman, Paulina. You're like a mother to me. A grandmother to my children. There's not an evil bone in your body. So forget all that mess Kevin said to you. All that matters is that I believe you had nothing to do with the kids getting taken."

"Well, I appreciate that, Mrs. Frost. That means so much to me," Paulina expressed.

"No need for that, Paulina. You're my rock and we're gonna ride for one another, okay?"

"Okay," she agreed, and finally smiled. "I couldn't say it earlier, but you sure ripped Mr. Frost a new one," she commented, smiling bashfully.

I smiled back at her. "I'm sure he didn't see it coming."

She smirked. "You should've seen his face."

"I can imagine," I replied.

"So, are you going to divorce him?"

"I will, after I get my babies back and all of this is over."

"Does he know this?"

"He will, soon enough," I told her while shaking my head with disgust, and thinking to myself he's about to have one rude awakening.

"So, what about the woman?" Paulina asked.

"What about her?"

"Do you think you'll ever get a chance to see her, face-to-face?"

"For what?"

"Don't you want to talk to her?"

"And say what to her?" I wondered aloud.

"Ask her why she's okay with sleeping with a married man who has a family," Paulina suggested.

"Kevin wouldn't dare give me the opportunity to speak with her."

"Why wait for him to give you the opportunity? Just take it."

"You mean, call her from his phone?"

"Yeah, or either get her number or call her from your own."

I thought for a second about what Paulina said and it piqued my interest. I already knew how she looked from the photo of her lying in the hospital bed. Not too flattering, if you want to know the truth. I mean, if you're going to cheat, do it with someone who looks better than the person you're already with. But as far as picking her brain about why she'd entertain my husband, after knowing he had a family, that had been put at the top of my list. I definitely wanted to know.

But what if she got smart with me and told me something that I didn't want to hear? I knew this would send me into a frenzy and would throw me off track from everything that's going on around here. To be perfectly honest, I'd probably hop in my car, take a drive to her house, and invite her ass outside. Then I'd start dragging her through the mud. I might even take her head off in the process. When you're in a fit of rage, you're liable to do anything. And in this case anything is possible. So it's probably best that I stay clear from that whore, or she could come up missing.

CHAPTER 18

Little Kevin and Kammy

"THINK WE'RE EVER GONNA SEE MOM AND DAD AGAIN?" KAMMY asked her brother.

"Yeah, we are," he assured her.

"I don't think so."

"Well, I do, so stop saying that."

Kammy's questions continued. "Think the police are looking for us?"

"Of course, they are."

"Do you think the man that brings us food is going to hurt us?" Kammy wondered out loud.

"I don't think he is," Little Kevin replied.

"Why you say that?" Kammy wanted to know.

"Because if he was, he would've done it by now."

"Do you think he's nice?"

"He's all right."

"Think he'll let us call Mom and Dad?"

Before Little Kevin could answer Kammy's question, the door to the soundproof basement opened and in came the masked man dressed all in black. He was carrying two bags of Chick-fil-A. Kammy got excited. "Is that for us?"

"Yes, it is."

"Do I have a toy?"

Little Kev nudged her.

"Oww . . ." Kammy whined out loud as she massaged her arm with her hand.

"I brought you guys something to eat," the man said, hoping he could cheer her up.

Little Kevin changed the subject. "Hey, can we call our parents?"

"I'm sorry, kid, but you can't," the guy told him.

"Why?" Kammy wanted to know.

"It's complicated. But don't worry, you'll see them soon enough," the guy assured them.

"When is that?" Kammy pressed him.

"Hopefully, in two days," the guy continued while placing both bags of food on the end of the bed that both kids shared.

"Are we ever gonna see your face?" Kammy blurted out unexpectedly.

The guy chuckled. "I'm afraid not."

"Why not?" Little Kevin asked.

"Because that's the way it has to be," the guy told them. Then without giving them a chance to question him further, he exited the room.

"Asshole!" Little Kevin mumbled.

"Ooooh, I'm telling," Kammy threatened.

Little Kevin nudged Kammy again. "Who are you gonna tell?"

"Ouch!" she whined from the push of Kevin's nudge.

"Shut up and eat your food," Little Kevin instructed her, grabbing one of the bags of Chick-fil-A.

They both sat on the edge of the bed and started eating the food the guy left them. "Did you believe him when he said that we were going to see Mommy and Daddy soon?" Kammy asked between chews.

"If we don't, I'm gon' break us out of here."

"How you gon' do that?" Kammy wanted to know.

"You'll see," Little Kevin said confidently, and then he continued eating.

CHAPTER 19

Kevin

I SWEAR, I DREADED GOING HOME TO FACE AVA. BUT I KNEW I COULDN'T avoid her forever. We shared a house together, and I needed to check in to see if she'd heard anything about the kids. As soon as I entered my house, I looked for Ava and found her in our bedroom. She was looking through a photo book she put together of pictures of the kids. She gave me an evil stare as I stood at the entryway of the bedroom. "Well, hello to you." I spoke despite the fact I knew she wasn't going to speak back.

"What do you want?" she asked sharply.

"Heard anything from the kidnappers?" I asked.

"If I did, I would've called you," she replied sarcastically as she continued to look through the book of photos.

I entered the room and closed the door so I could speak with her in private. I saw Ava watching me through her peripheral vision, but still holding her attention on the photos before her.

"I know you don't believe that Paulina let the kidnappers in the house, but something just doesn't sit right with me about this whole thing," I pointed out.

"Well, I don't care what doesn't sit right with you. I know for a fact that didn't happen."

"And how do you know that?"

"Because I know her, and I know she wouldn't do anything like that."

"Then tell me how the kidnappers got in here without breaking a window or any of the locks? It looks like it was an inside job."

"I don't care what it looks like. I know Paulina didn't do it," Ava insisted.

"But what if she did?" I protested as I stood before the bed.

"Stop saying that."

"Why? Because you don't wanna face the truth?"

"What truth are you talking about, Kevin? Because the truth I wanna hear, you've done your best to steer clear of," she spat out with a deep anger in her voice.

I backed down by saying, "Come on now, Ava, don't start." I wasn't trying to argue with her right now. I just wanted her to see my side of things concerning how the kidnappers broke into the house, but I saw she wasn't trying to go there.

"That's funny that you wanna talk about everything except for your fucking mistress and that fucking bastard-ass baby of yours."

"We already talked about it. You know everything," I reminded her.

"I know your side. Now I wanna hear her side," she said.

Panic shot through my heart after hearing Ava tell me that she wanted to hear Ty's side of the story. Was she crazy? Ty would surely give Ava an earful of our intimate exploits, damaging any chance of reconciliation, and I couldn't let that happen. How could I tell her no without her going off the deep end?

"So, are you just gonna stand there and look stupid? Get her on the phone right now," Ava pressed me.

"I'm not calling her," I said adamantly.

She took the book of photos off her lap and placed them next to her as she gave me a menacing look. I could tell that she was ready to go to war with me.

"What do you have to hide?" she asked.

I knew that it was a trick question. How to answer it, I didn't know.

"Cat got your tongue?" she continued, her voice sounding mechanical as she moved her body toward the edge of the bed. She was definitely coming for me. I could see it in her eyes.

"No," I finally answered her.

"So you're telling me that you're not calling her?" she asked again. Then she rose to her feet and stood before me defiantly.

Up until now, Ava had never approached me in this manner. I knew she had an aggressive side to her, but never to this extent. But then I realized, I'd never put her in this situation before, either. So I figured it would be best to defuse this hairy situation before it really went south.

"I'm not gonna do this with you," I said while backing away from her.

"After we get the kids back, I'm filing for divorce," she blurted out point-blank.

An instant gut punch dazed me mentally for a couple of seconds as I exited the bedroom. As prepared as I thought I would be when I finally heard those words, I wasn't. My life was crumbling before my very eyes. The whole family unit I had built with Ava would no longer be the same after today, and now I had to come to terms with it—whether I wanted to or not.

The messed-up part about it is that it was all my fault. I created this shit. I went out, had an extramarital affair, got the woman pregnant, and here we are.

CHAPTER 20

Ava

Watching Kevin leave our bedroom, doing the walk of shame, gave me so much pleasure, even though he didn't act the way I thought he would. In my mind I imagined him putting up a fight and telling me that we weren't going to break up the family. Unfortunately, that just wasn't the case. It appeared he had completely checked out of the relationship. Maybe he was waiting for me to find out about the affair so that I could pull the plug and he wouldn't look like the bad guy in front of the kids. If that's the case, then he beat me to the punch.

I started to follow him to wherever he was going, but I decided to abort the mission. I didn't want to give him the satisfaction that I was running after him like a scorned teenage girl. If anything, that bastard should've been running behind me, kissing my ass, and telling me how sorry he was for doing this to our family. But no, it seemed as though he'd rather do the latter. Maybe this new chick had some kind of hold on him.

Whatever it is, I will find out, and it will be sooner than later. Just as soon as that fucker falls to sleep, I'm going to take his phone and call her myself. I'm gonna get to the bottom of this.

While planning in my head what I was going to say to this

woman, it dawned on me that I didn't have to wait on Kevin to go to sleep. He and I were on the same phone plan, so I had access to every number he has ever called. In order to get this number, all I had to do was log into our cell phone account and, voila, it would be listed there.

Without further hesitation I grabbed my laptop from my nightstand, climbed back on my bed, and logged onto our cellular provider's website. After I keyed in my user ID number and password, I was in. *Boom!* My heart rate instantly picked up speed as soon as the homepage of my account popped up. It read: Welcome Ava Frost. Anxiety began to consume me as I searched the top menu for the bill or call log information. After three short seconds I located it and clicked on it. My and Kevin's call log summary, divided into two separate columns, was in full view. I clicked on his list and saw a ton of phone numbers. What stuck out to me was an 804 number that Kevin called frequently. The person who owned the number seemed to call Kevin more frequently, though, and I noticed that the calls even came at odd times of the night. This was the mistress, no doubt, so I grabbed my cell phone from my nightstand and dialed the number.

Immediately after the phone started ringing, my adrenaline started pumping. It felt like I was gearing up for a boxing match. Thoughts of what I was going to say to her started surfacing in my mind. Then I started thinking about what she was going to say in return. Was she going to be nice, apologetic, or belligerent? Before I could get an idea of how I was going to approach this situation, she answered.

"Hello," I heard her say. Her voice was warm, soft, and gentle. A bit Southern, I might add.

"Hello, Ty," I replied confidently. I wanted to sound superior and give her the impression that I wasn't on the phone to play games with her.

"Who is this?" she asked. But there was no doubt in my mind

that she knew who I was. I wanted to call her out about it, but I left well enough alone and moved right along.

"It's Kevin's wife," I told her boldly.

"What a surprise," she commented. I could hear her country accent more definitively and she also sounded like she was somewhat educated.

"It shouldn't be; you're screwing my husband," I added.

"Look, if you called to curse me out—"

I cut her off in midsentence. "No, I didn't call to curse you out. I called to find out how long have you been sleeping with my husband."

"He didn't tell you?" she said sarcastically.

Her reaction, of course, struck a nerve. So I came back stronger and said, "No, but when I confronted him about you, he did tell me that you were a jump-off. Someone he fucked on the first night and you got pregnant. Then out of respect for the baby, he decided to remain cool with you."

"I wasn't no fucking jump-off! And we didn't fuck on the first night. We dated for a couple of weeks before I slept with him!" she roared back at me. And *boom,* just like that, I hit her nerve. I chuckled softly so she wouldn't hear me. But I must admit that it felt good to send this bitch into a fit of rage. It felt so good to show her how it feels to be fucked with.

"Well, I wonder why he's denying having a relationship with you?" I replied nonchalantly, pulling her further in. I knew that by insinuating he was denying having had a relationship with her, she'd be furious and tell me everything.

"I don't know what he's told you, but we've been together for close to two years now. We met while he was on a connecting flight from New York. We exchanged numbers and started talking from time to time. Then he drove out to Richmond to hang out with me for the weekend. After we hit it off, we decided to keep in touch and see where it would go. Fast-forward to now.

Here we are, we have a beautiful three-month-old little girl, and he just bought us a new house."

"You say all of that like he's a single man. It didn't bother you that he was married with a family?"

"He didn't tell me he was married until after we had sex," she volunteered.

"And even then, it didn't bother you?"

"It did at first. But when he'd tell me that you guys were starting not to get along and were on the verge of getting a divorce, I saw my opportunity to make a family with him."

"So you were just waiting in the cut, huh?"

She became defensive. "What do you mean by that?"

"It means that you were waiting for the right time to break up my home," I snapped.

"What makes you think your home was solid in the beginning? He told me that when you and him first got together, you had just gotten out of a relationship with his best friend. So, if you want my opinion, your situation ain't no better. You slept with the homie, got knocked up, and that's the only reason why he wifed you up," she tossed back.

Furious by this woman's verbal insults, I flew into a rage. I mean, how the fuck did she know that I had a relationship with Kevin's best friend before he and I had gotten together? Not to mention, she knew I had gotten pregnant with my son before Kevin and I had tied the knot. Now what kind of bullshit is that? Does he have her thinking that I trapped him into this marriage? And if so, does he really feel like that? Even if he didn't, why tell her? Now this bitch has something over my head. That fucking pillow talk will get an adulterer to talk every time.

"Listen, I don't know what he told you, but I didn't sleep with the homie. It wasn't one of those type of parties," I lied.

Now, I can't tell you why I denied being with Nick, because it's nothing to be ashamed of, especially since he and I had been together for a long time. Not only that, Kevin pursued me. He brought kids and marriage up to me. It was his idea, not mine, so to have this ho thinking that I got pregnant and purposely trapped him into marrying me is a slap in the face.

"Well, whatever type of party it was, I'm no worse than you," she made it a point to say.

I wasted no time in insulting her back. "Bitch, you slept with a married man, and a bastard baby came out of it."

"My baby ain't no bastard!"

"Then what do you call a side chick having a baby with a married man? What? Illegitimate? Either way, if anything happened to my husband, you and your baby won't get shit. But me and my kids would be entitled to everything," I said with a chuckle.

"That is, if you get your kids back," she blurted out boldly.

Taken aback by her outburst, I felt my heart sink into the pit of my stomach. The fact that she knew about the kids being kidnapped said a lot about how much Kevin trusted her.

I mean, does he know that by telling her it could potentially derail my plans of getting my kids back? Because what if she gets up the gumption to tell the cops or someone else, for that matter? No one is supposed to know, and Kevin violated that.

I swear, I will fucking kill him myself if the cops find out, and the kidnappers get wind of it.

"Let me tell you something, you fucking slut!" I snarled at her. "I know you would love for me not to ever see my kids again so your baby could have Kevin alone. You wicked-ass bitch! But I will see them again, and when I do, you will be the first to know. Before I get off this phone with you, I'm telling you right now that if you ever speak ill of my children again, I will personally come and pay you a visit," I threatened her.

"Who are you talking to?" Kevin asked after he walked back into the bedroom.

"I'm talking to your side bitch!" I roared. Then I pressed the SPEAKER button so that she could hear Kevin's voice, and vice versa.

"I'm not his side bitch!" she shouted.

"Ty, hang up the phone right now!" Kevin shouted to her.

"No, fuck that, Kevin, you told her about the kids!" I yelled.

Kevin stood there dumbfounded. "She promised not to say anything," he finally said.

Disgusted by his admission, I said, "Wait, so you're having pillow talk with your side bitch?"

"I'm not his side bitch!" she commented again.

"Shut up, ho! You are a fucking side bitch! And you will also be a dead bitch if you utter one word to the cops about my children," I hissed.

"You . . ." she started saying, but I pressed the END button, stopping her in midsentence. Then I looked up from the phone and gave Kevin the look of death. The anger and rage inside of me wanted to rip his face off. The fact that he betrayed not only me, but the safety of our children, was on a whole other level. He put our children's lives in a compromising position. She meant that much to him that he had to go and tell her?

I stood there in utter disbelief. "Why? Why would you tell her after I told you not to say anything to anyone?" Tears began to build up in my eyes.

"I didn't mean to. You called while I was with her, and she heard the conversation," he explained.

"Oh, so I caught you in the middle of fucking her, huh?" I replied sarcastically. By now, tears were running down my face.

"No, Ava, we weren't. I was actually asleep when you called."

"I'm telling you right now, if that bitch calls and tells anyone, and the kidnappers find out, I will kill you and her both!" I made that clear before storming off into the bathroom.

"Ava, I am so sorry!" Kevin shouted loud enough for me to hear.

But his words fell on deaf ears, and I kept going.

CHAPTER 21

Ty

"WAIT, NO, THIS BITCH DIDN'T JUST HANG UP ON ME!" I GRIPED as I looked down at my phone. "And then to hear her disrespect me, and Kevin didn't jump to my defense, is a slap in the face. Oh, he definitely has some explaining to do right now," I huffed while dialing his cell phone number. I stood there and listened to it ring five times without an answer. Pissed off, I dialed his number again and allowed it to ring six times, but once again he didn't answer. "They must be arguing," I said aloud, taking the phone away from my ear.

Filled with anxiety, I needed someone to vent to, so I called my homegirl Whitney and prayed that she answered. After the third ring, she did.

"Hey, girl, what's up?"

"Girl, you aren't gonna believe what just happened."

"What?"

"Do you know that Kevin's wife just called me?"

"Really? What did she say?"

"This bitch had the nerve to insinuate that I was a home-wrecker and ask me why I would mess around with Kevin knowing he was married?" I stated.

"And what did you say?"

"I told her that he said the marriage was already on the rocks, so that's why I stuck around."

"And what did she say after that?"

"She started going off the deep end, calling me a side bitch—"

"Oh no, she didn't," Whitney declared.

"Yes, that bitch did, but I shut her ass down when I burst her bubble by telling her that I knew about her kids getting kidnapped."

"Wait, what?" Whitney asked.

"You heard me. Kevin's kids were kidnapped on Wednesday, and his wife is mad because he told me about it."

"Fuck being mad about you knowing, did they get them back yet?" she wanted to know.

"No. They have to give the kidnappers a two-million-dollar ransom."

Taken aback by my statement, Whitney shouted, "Two million!"

"Yup, and they don't have the money. Fucking stupid bitch! Talking all that shit to me. I've got my baby right here, safe and sound. She needs to try to figure out how to get her kids back," I commented sarcastically.

Whitney seemed concerned. "Oh, my God! What are they going to do?"

"I don't know, and I don't care," I answered back.

"That's not nice, Ty," Whitney said to me.

"What do you mean *that's not nice?* So you're taking up for that bitch?"

"No, I'm not. But the fact that their kids got kidnapped is serious. What are the cops saying?"

"They didn't call 'em."

"Why not?"

"Because the kidnappers told them not to."

"Are they crazy? I would've called the cops as soon as I found out they were gone," Whitney asserted.

"I would've done the same thing. Look at who we're talking about. She's a fucking know-it-all. And on top of that, she's rude as fuck. So, I say, she gets what she deserves," I said.

"Nah, I don't wish that on no one. I say, you would call the cops and report it yourself," Whitney suggested.

"For what?" I screeched. "They aren't my kids. And besides, I really couldn't care less," I admitted.

She tried to reason with me. "Well, what's their names? I'll call 'em. I mean, someone with some sense needs to let the cops know what's going on. Those kids could be in a world of danger. God knows what those people are doing to those poor kids."

"I'm sorry, but that's not my problem," I responded. But to be honest, I really couldn't care less. I was glad that their kids were gone. Now Kevin could focus solely on my baby.

"What's the kids' names?" she asked me again.

"Kammy and Little Kevin," I replied.

"What's Kevin's last name?"

"Why?" I questioned her. She surprised me with the back-to-back questions.

"Because if you don't care to call the police, I'll call 'em. Someone needs to call 'em."

"Call them and say what?"

"Tell them that someone kidnapped those children," Whitney explained.

"You don't even know what city they live in," I protested.

"You are going to tell me, right?"

"Girl, just drop it. That shit doesn't even concern us. That's their business, so let them handle it."

The fact that she wanted to meddle in Kevin and his wife's business was beyond me. I'm trying to figure out if she's on my side or Ava's. I only called her to vent about the run-in I had with Kevin's wife, but she seemed more concerned about the welfare of the kids than the argument I had. I didn't appreciate that at all.

Frustrated by this whole conversation, I figured it would be best to end the call. "Girl, let me call you later," I told her.

"But wait—" Whitney started to say, but I ended the call before she could finish.

After ending the call, I sat there for a moment and began to think about how I could get back at Ava. And then it came to me. My bestie was right. Someone needed to call the cops, but not in the way she intended. I figured that if I called the cops and reported the kidnapping, they would go to Kevin's house, do a welfare check, and find out that the kids were gone. Then, for sure, the cops would blow Kevin and his wife's spot up—and when the kidnappers found out about it, there's no doubt in my mind that they would never see their kids again. Now, that's revenge!

Without further hesitation I dialed 911 from my cell phone and got an operator on the line. "What is your emergency?" the woman asked.

"I would like to report a kidnapping," I said.

"Can you state your name, please?"

"I would like to remain anonymous," I told her.

The woman's questions continued. "Okay, so who was kidnapped, ma'am?"

"A very close friend of mine. The kidnapping took place in Virginia Beach, Virginia."

"Okay, ma'am, well, you're gonna have to hang up with me and call the local Virginia Beach Police Department and have them dispatch officers to the address of the victims."

"Okay, thank you," I said. Then I ended the call.

Immediately after I hung up with the 911 operator, I searched the number for the Virginia Beach Police Department from my cell phone and found four different precincts. I called the first one.

"You reached Virginia Beach's thirty-first zone," a man's voice said.

"Hi, sir, my name is Sonya," I started off, lying. "I have a question."

"How can I help you?"

"Okay, so I live in another city, but I just found out that a friend of mine's children were just kidnapped. They live in your city, but they refuse to report the crime, for fear that the kidnappers will hurt their children, so my question to you is, what would you do if you were me?" I said with concern.

"I would do just what you're doing," the man replied.

"Can I do it anonymously? I don't want it getting back to them that I was the one who called, if something went wrong."

"Sure, you can. Do you know the home address in which the crime took place?"

I thought for a moment about Kevin's home address, because I didn't know it offhand. Then it dawned on me that I had a copy of Kevin's driver's license in a folder that contained the documents from when we purchased the house.

"Yes, I do. Hold on a second," I said, rushing into Kevin's home office. I grabbed the folder from the small cabinet next to the desk.

I rustled through the paperwork while the police officer waited on the phone. After sifting through the stack of documents, I found it. "Okay, I have it," I acknowledged. "It's 1593 Rosebud Lane, Virginia Beach, Virginia, 23462," I responded.

The officer fell silent for a moment; then he said, "That address is out of my district, but I can transfer you to our local 911 operator and they can dispatch officers to go out to that residence."

"Okay."

"All right, hold while I transfer you."

"Thank you."

"You're welcome."

I heard a loud click, then a tiny ringing sound, and then another clicking sound. Seconds later, I heard a voice say, "Nine-one-one operator, what is your emergency?"

"I would like to report a kidnapping," I said.

"Your name, ma'am?"

"I would like to remain anonymous, if I can."

"Who was kidnapped, ma'am?" the woman asked while I heard her typing.

"A little girl and boy," I replied.

"What are their names?"

"Kammy and Kevin Frost."

"Are they related?" The woman's questions continued as she keyed in my answers.

"Yes, they're brother and sister."

"What's the address of where the children were taken?"

"It's 1593 Rosebud Lane, Virginia Beach, VA 23462," I recited.

"Do you know what time this crime happened?"

"Not sure of the time. But I do know that it was very early on Wednesday, before seven a.m.," I informed the woman.

"How do you know the children were kidnapped?"

"Because I know the parents of the children. They told me what happened, and they also said the kidnappers left a ransom note instructing them not to call the cops. But I told them that they should, but they refused to do it. So that's why I'm calling you."

"What are the names of the parents?"

"Kevin and Ava Frost."

"Now, are you sure that the children were kidnapped?"

"Yes, ma'am, I am positive."

"And you said that this kidnapping happened in the early-morning hours of Wednesday?"

"Yes, ma'am."

"And you also say the kidnappers left a ransom note behind?"

"Yes, ma'am."

"Did the parents tell you the ransom amount?"

"Yes, two million."

"Do you know if they've had contact with the kidnappers?"

"No, I'm not sure."

"Okay, no worries. I'm gonna send a patrol car over to that residence."

"Thank you."

"Have a nice day," she said before hanging up.

Immediately after I finished the call, I sat there and started smiling wickedly. I knew I had just pulled off the cleverest revenge plot of a lifetime. Let's see how Ava gets her way out of this sticky situation. Because from the way I see it, when the cops arrive at her place, they're gonna blow her whole spot up. And guess what that means? The kidnappers will definitely find out about it, and then she and Kevin will never see their kids again. Boom! Plan well devised and executed. Bet you she'll think about how she talks to me the next time!

CHAPTER 22

Kevin

I WAS LYING ON THE SOFA WATCHING TV WHEN I HEARD THE DOORbell ring. *Ding-dong! Ding-dong!* It startled me for a second because I wasn't expecting any visitors. But I got up to see who it was. "Who is it?" I yelled as I made my way to the front door. I heard a reply, but it was barely audible. I figured I was too far away from the door, so I continued forward.

Ava heard the doorbell ring, too, because while I wondered who was at the front door, she was making her way out of the bedroom and down the staircase.

"Who is it?" I heard her say.

"I'm trying to figure that out now," I told her after looking back over my shoulder.

"Is this the residence of Kevin and Ava Frost?" a male's voice asked from the other side of the front door.

Curious to see to whom this voice belonged, I opened the front door. Shocked to see that it was two Black cops, I gasped, but I tried to hold it together.

"How can I help you?" I asked both uniformed police officers, and then Ava joined me at the front door.

"Are you Kevin Frost?" the police officer asked me.

"Yes, I am," I replied reluctantly.

"Well, my name is Officer Perry, and this is Officer King," he started off saying.

"Okay, Officer Perry, what is this about?" Ava asked, standing alongside me.

"We received a call about a kidnapping," Officer Perry announced.

Surprised by his statement, I looked back at Ava for some assistance.

"What kidnapping?" she blurted out.

"We've received a call that your children, Kammy and Kevin Frost, were kidnapped sometime early yesterday," he explained.

"I don't know who could've told you that, but that's not true," Ava continued.

Officer Perry pressed the issue. "Are those children yours?"

"Yes," Ava answered.

"Are they here?" Officer Perry wanted to know.

"No," Ava responded.

"Then where are they?" Officer King interjected.

"They're with my parents," Ava quickly said.

"Where are your parents?" Officer King asked her.

"Home."

"Could you get them on the phone so that we could do a welfare check?" Officer Perry joined back in.

Ava froze instantly. I could tell that she didn't know what to do, so I threw her a lifeline. "Go get your phone and call them," I instructed her. She hesitated for a second, as if she didn't know what to do. I nudged her. "Just go and get your phone," I repeated.

"Can we come in and wait while she makes the call?" Officer Perry asked nicely.

"Yeah, sure," I said, but in actuality I didn't want those motherfuckers coming in my house. But I figured that if I refused to cooperate, I'd look suspicious, and they'd really ride my ass.

"Is there anyone else in the house besides you two?" Officer Perry asked as he proceeded into the house. His partner, Officer King, eyed every inch of the foyer and the hallway as he followed him into my home.

"Yes, our housekeeper is here," I replied as calmly as I could, but at the same time wondered why he wanted to know who else was in the house.

"Can you tell her to come down here, please?" he added.

"Yeah, sure," I said reluctantly. Now I was really starting to worry. Did he want Paulina down here to grill her about the kids? To see if they were really kidnapped or not? Or was this just a safety precaution they needed to take while they were in my home? Either way I didn't like it one bit.

"Hey, Ava," I shouted her name as she walked toward the staircase.

"Yeah," she shouted back, peering from around the corner of the bedroom door.

"Would you tell Paulina to come downstairs?" I asked.

Ava gave me this odd look. It was an expression of dread and fear, and then she turned her head and walked away. I stood there, not knowing what to do, until Officer King started probing me with more questions.

"So, how long have your children been in the custody of the grandparents?" he asked.

I turned around and faced him. "I was out of town when they were picked up, so you're gonna have to ask my wife."

"Why were you out of town, if you don't mind me asking?" His questions continued.

"Business trip," I said flatly.

"What's taking her so long to get the housekeeper?" Officer King interjected.

I hunched my shoulders. "I don't know, maybe she was asleep," I replied, turning my attention back toward the staircase. "Ava, is Paulina asleep?" I shouted loud enough so that she could hear me.

"We're coming now, Kevin," she responded, and then seconds later, she appeared before our eyes. Paulina was in tow. When she laid eyes on the police officers standing next to me, she smiled nervously.

"You're the housekeeper?" Officer Perry asked.

Paulina nodded.

"Can you come down here for a moment? And, Mrs. Frost, would you come with her so that you can make that call for us?" he added.

"Sure," Ava agreed.

I watched as she and Paulina walked down the stairs, and so did the police officers. When Ava and Paulina made it downstairs, the cops immediately took control of the room.

"Can you get the grandparents on the phone, please?" Officer Perry pressed the issue.

Instantly I saw sweat pellets seeping out of Ava's pores, but she was still trying to hold it together. She held her cell phone before her and proceeded to dial her father's number. I was pretty sure that she was calling him. She stared at the phone screen hard and then she abruptly pressed the END button. She chuckled nervously and said, "My bad, I was dialing the wrong number."

Then she started going through her contact list, and when she landed on the cell phone number she was looking for, she tapped on it. The phone lit up and then it started ringing. I knew then she was trying to avoid getting her dad on the phone, so she called her mother, who she knew wasn't going to answer, since she had dementia.

The call rang five times before the voicemail picked up. "Oh, she's not answering," Ava announced in front of us.

"Try again," Officer Perry instructed her.

"Can we all have a seat?" I suggested. I was tired of all of us standing around.

"Yeah, sure," Officer Perry agreed.

Ava, Paulina, and I walked over to the living-room sofa and took a seat. Meanwhile, Ava was still pretending to get her mother on the phone. After the phone started ringing, it rang for several times, then went straight to voicemail.

"She's not answering," Ava told the officers again.

"What's the home address? We'll have a unit go over and do a welfare check," Officer King said.

Panic stricken, I stood there, not knowing what to do or say.

Ava blurted out, "Is that even necessary?"

"Well, I'm afraid it is, ma'am," Officer King said.

"Why is that?" I interjected.

"It's like this: anytime we get a call from an anonymous party stating there's been a kidnapping and we come to the residence and the children aren't present, then we have to find out where they are," he explained.

"And you just can't take our word for it?" I added.

"No, I'm sorry, but we can't," Officer King responded.

"Why don't you just give us your parents' home address so we can send a unit over there, and when they get there and tell us that your children are safe, we'll be out of your hair," Officer Perry chimed back in.

"But what if we refuse to do so?" I wanted to know.

"Then we'll call backup and report your children missing," Officer Perry stated.

"But they're not missing," Ava argued.

"And to make sure of that, we have to do a welfare check," Officer Perry insisted.

Ava let out a long sigh and shook her head with disgust. "I wish I knew who called you guys. I swear, I would call them and curse them out. Got you around here wasting my time," Ava grumbled.

"Like I said, if you give us your parents' home address, we can have a unit over there in no time to do a welfare check. Once they tell us that everything is fine, and the children are safe, we'll be out of here," Officer Perry reiterated.

Ava sat there on the sofa, with her arms folded in protest, so the cops looked at me. I hunched my shoulders and said, "I don't know their address. I just know how to get there," I announced. I only said it to get the heat off me, but I could tell they weren't buying into it.

"So, what's it gonna be, Mrs. Frost?" Officer King chimed back in.

She sat there quietly, giving them the evil eye. Officer Perry grabbed his partner by the arm and said, "Let me talk to you privately for a moment." Then they both stepped off and walked to the other side of the room, but they kept their eyes on us. While they were in their huddle, Officer Perry started whispering so that only Officer King could hear him.

This infuriated Ava and she said something. "It's rude to whisper, and especially in someone else's house," she complained.

Officer Perry lifted his hand. "We'll be with you in a moment," he assured her.

But I knew his hand gesture really meant for her to close her mouth.

"I don't like this one bit," Paulina whispered.

"Wait, hold up, what did you say?" Officer King asked as he stepped away from his partner and started walking back in our direction. His partner followed.

Paulina's mouth dropped open, and she instantly clammed up. She looked at Ava and me for guidance, but Officer King scolded her. "Don't look at them. Look at me and tell me what you just said."

"Don't talk to her like that!" Ava snapped.

Paulina looked timidly at the cops.

"Paulina, you don't have to talk to them," Ava said aggressively.

120

"You shut up right now, Mrs. Frost," Officer King ordered.

"Hey, wait! You can't talk to my wife like that," I spoke up.

"Yeah, you don't talk to me like that!" Ava shouted.

Officer Perry threw both of his hands in the air to get everyone's attention. "Everybody, calm down!" he yelled.

"What do you mean, 'calm down'? This is my house," Ava snapped.

Officer Perry ignored Ava and directed his attention toward Paulina. "Ma'am, where are you from?" he asked.

"Mexico," Paulina responded.

"Are you here legally?" he continued.

"What kind of question is that? Of course, she is," Ava interjected.

"I'm talking to her, ma'am," Officer Perry told Ava as he shot her a harsh look.

Paulina nodded. "Yes, I have my papers," she acknowledged.

"Okay, can you please come with me?" he asked her respectfully.

Paulina nodded her head. "Sure," she said.

"You don't have to go with him," Ava told Paulina.

Officer Perry continued to ignore Ava's remarks and held his hand out for Paulina to grab. Then he helped her up from the sofa.

"Where are you taking her?" Ava asked.

I could practically see fireballs shooting out of her eyes.

Officer King stepped in. "Mrs. Frost, I'm gonna ask you to please let us do our job."

"But this is my house," she protested.

"I understand that, but we're here now and we have an obligation to do our job. As soon as you let us do that, we'll be out of your hair," Officer King assured her.

"Do you realize that we didn't have to let you into our house?" she pointed out.

"If you hadn't let us in, we would have gotten a court order that would've allowed us to gain entry," he said with cockiness.

"Did you hear that shit, Kevin? See, when you let these mother-fuckers in your house, they take over. Next time we'll wait for a court order," Ava hissed.

Then she turned her attention in the direction where the other officer had taken Paulina. We both noticed that he had taken her into the kitchen. We sat there, for what seemed like forever, as Officer Perry questioned her about God knows what. In my mind I knew it had to be about the kids' whereabouts, so I hoped that Ava had coached her beforehand. I kept my fingers crossed that Paulina knew what to say to the officer. Otherwise, we'd all be fucked.

"Why is it taking them so long?" Ava questioned Officer King.

"Don't worry! They'll be back in a moment," he told her.

Ava wouldn't let up. "What is he asking her?"

"That's none of your concern right now," he replied force-fully.

"She's my housekeeper. I'm responsible for her," Ava an-swered back.

"She's a grown woman, Mrs. Frost."

"So that means she doesn't have to answer his questions if she doesn't want to," Ava remarked. "Paulina, don't answer any of his questions!" Ava shouted from where she was standing.

"Mrs. Frost, if you make another outburst like that, I'm gonna—"

Before he could finish, Ava cut him off in midsentence. "You're gonna have to do what? Arrest me?" She chuckled. "I'd like to see you try it."

"Mr. Frost, will you calm your wife down, please?" he asked me.

"Or what? I'm a grown woman. Can't no one make me calm down, but me." She continued to be combative.

Thankfully, Officer Perry and Paulina came walking out of

the kitchen. Paulina expressed nervousness. Ava quickly took notice of it and immediately started to question her.

"Paulina, what did he say to you?" Ava asked her.

"I wanna keep them separated," Officer Perry told his partner.

"Okay," he replied. "Ma'am, sit over there on the other couch, please," Officer King instructed Paulina.

"Why can't she sit where she was sitting before?" Ava wanted to know.

"It's for our safety, ma'am," Officer King answered.

"Paulina, what did he ask you?" Ava pressed the issue.

Paulina carefully walked by us and whispered the words "I'm sorry." Then she took a seat on the sofa on the other side of the room. It was catercorner to us, so we could see the side of her face as she looked down into her lap.

"What did you say to her?" Ava roared.

"Calm down, Ava," I said, grabbing her hand.

She snatched it away from me. "Tell me what you said to her?" she griped.

Officer Perry whispered something in Officer King's ear, and then Officer King stepped away and headed toward the front door. As he exited my home, I heard him talking into the radio attached to his shoulder.

"Dispatch, I have a 134. Can you send backup?" I heard him say.

"What is a 134?" Ava asked Officer Perry, who was now standing in the middle of the living-room floor like he was monitoring our every move.

"My partner is calling for backup," Officer Perry announced.

"'Backup'!" she shouted.

"For what?" I yelled. But I knew then that Paulina had told the cop everything about the kidnapping.

"Cut it out, you guys. We know what's going on, so what you better do is start cooperating before the FBI is brought in."

A sharp pain of panic raced through my heart when he said FBI. They were the big shots, and I knew once they got involved, they were going to bring a huge presence—and the kidnappers were surely going to find out. Everything from there was surely going downhill.

"Listen, you don't understand what you're doing," I started to say.

"Shut up, Kevin! Don't say another word," Ava warned me.

I barked at her, "No, you shut up!" Then I turned my attention back toward the officer. "You guys are gonna fuck shit up if you call for backup. We don't need your help. If we did, we would've called you in the first place," I pointed out.

"I'm sorry, Mr. Frost, but it's out of my hands now," Officer Perry replied apologetically. But it was all bullshit.

"If those motherfuckers kill our kids because you put your nose where it didn't belong, I'm coming after you personally," Ava threatened him.

"I'm sorry you feel that way, Mrs. Frost."

"Sorry, my ass! Fuck you!" she screeched, and then she shot up from the sofa.

"Have a seat, Mrs. Frost," Officer Perry told her.

"Am I under arrest?" she asked him.

"No."

"Well, then, I don't have to keep sitting down. This is my freaking house. I can go where I please."

"Is that really necessary?" I asked Officer Perry. I mean, for God's sake, we were in our home, and where would she go?

Ava ignored the cop and proceeded into the bathroom that was a few feet away from the sofa.

"Look, I just wanna keep an eye on everyone until backup gets here," he stated.

"Well, as you can see, she's only going to the bathroom," I pointed out.

"Yeah, I see, but just make sure she comes back and takes a seat when she's done."

I let out a long sigh. "Hey, listen, Officer, will you just lighten up a bit? We've been through enough yesterday and today, so I don't want her feeling like she's a prisoner in her own home," I said.

He thought for a second before speaking. "All right, but just make sure that she doesn't leave the house," he negotiated with me.

"You got it," I assured him, and then I stood up from the sofa. He stopped me before I walked off.

"Before your wife comes back, why don't you tell me what really happened?"

I stood there for a second and looked him in the eyes. I wanted him to know that every word I was about to utter was coming from the heart of a man who loves his children, and that I would do anything for them, even if it meant putting my own life on the line. "Look, I was out of town when I got the call from my wife telling me that my kids had been kidnapped, and the kidnappers left a ransom note demanding two million dollars. They clearly told us that if we called the cops, they would kill my babies. Now, do you know how helpless that made us feel? We wanted to call you guys, but we were afraid to do so."

"I understand," Officer Perry said.

"So you're saying that you would've done the same thing?"

"I can't say. But what I can say is I respect your decision to try to do whatever you felt was necessary to protect your kids."

"I appreciate that. But let me ask you."

"Yeah."

"What's gonna happen now?"

"Well, we've dispatched detectives from our Special Victims Unit to come out and speak with you. After doing so, they'll make a determination if they are going to bring the Feds in on it."

"Oh no! We can't bring in the FBI. The kidnappers will surely find out and we'll never see our kids again!" I felt panicked.

"Don't worry, we're going to be very careful and quiet," Officer Perry assured me.

"I hope so," I said, exhaling deeply. I was becoming extremely overwhelmed by this whole ordeal. To know that detectives were on their way to my home to talk to Ava and me gave me anxiety. I swear, I didn't want anything wrong to happen and the kidnappers to find out that we were talking to the cops. Somehow we had to figure out a way to keep this under lock and key.

CHAPTER 23

Ava

I DREADED WALKING OUT OF THE BATHROOM. I DIDN'T WANT TO FACE the cops anymore. I wanted them to leave my house at once. They were going to mess around and alert the kidnappers. I swore I would lose my damn mind if something happened to my children. Then, on top of that, they interrogated my house-keeper, Paulina, in the kitchen. They cornered her and made her tell them everything they wanted to know. How could she let them manipulate her like that? I was so mad.

What's so hurtful is that she betrayed me. She allowed them to get in her head and convince her to go against me. I've always looked at her as family, and now I was questioning her loyalty to me. I mean, did she know what she just did? All she had to do was keep her mouth shut, but she didn't. She had to go and blab her mouth about the kidnapping and now my kids' safety could be in jeopardy. But what I really wanted to know is, who called the cops in the first place? Who alerted them about the kidnapping in the first place?

The only people outside of this house who knew about our situation was Nick, and my dad. But wait. Kevin's side bitch knew about it, too. So, what if she was the one who called? She had plenty of motive to do it. I mean, I did just curse her out. This could be the perfect way of getting back at me without me knowing. The question is: Does she know where Kevin and I live? Has he brought her here before? I swear, if he has, I'll sure make him pay dearly for it. And her, too, for that matter. Now I had to figure out, what was I going to do? As a matter of fact, what was going to happen next?

After a few minutes of gathering my thoughts, I mustered up the energy to exit the bathroom and reenter the living room, where my husband, Paulina, and the cops were waiting for me.

"Are you okay?" Kevin asked me.

The sight of him repulsed me and I wanted to lash out on him at that very moment, but I held my composure and rolled my eyes at him. I turned my attention toward the cops and asked them, what was going to happen next?

"Well, we're waiting for our detectives from the Special Victims Unit to stop by, and then they'll be able to lay out everything for you and take things from there," Officer King explained.

"So there's no way that we can handle this without detectives coming here?" I wanted to know.

"No, I'm afraid not," Officer King confirmed.

I immediately lost my cool. "I swear to God! If I lose my fucking children because y'all want to create a circus and have a bunch of cops show up at my door, there's gonna be hell to pay," I roared.

"Ava, please calm down," Kevin said as he tried to gently grab my hand.

I snatched my hand away. My voice boomed. "Don't touch me. Your fucking girlfriend probably is the one who called 'em."

Taken aback by my assertion, Kevin stepped backward and then turned around and walked away. I guess he got the hint that it was best to get away from me before I spazzed out on him.

"Who is this girlfriend?" Officer Perry wanted to know.

I chuckled. "I just found out yesterday that he has some woman and a child who live outside of Richmond. So it wouldn't shock me if she was the one who made the call to you guys."

"Think she may have had something to do with the kidnapping?" Officer Perry asked.

"It wouldn't surprise me. Because if she was the person who sent you guys here, then she knows where we live."

"That's bullshit, Ava! She wouldn't do that," Kevin asserted as he stormed back in our direction.

"And how do you know that?" I spat out.

"Because I know she's not that type of person."

"Well, then, tell me who called these people? Who? Nick? My dad?"

"I don't know," Kevin answered.

"Oh, fuck off! You know. She's the only one who would do something like this," I made clear.

"Calm down, ma'am," Officer Perry suggested.

"I'm calm. This pussy-whipped asshole here needs to open his eyes," I retorted.

"I'm not pussy whipped," Kevin refuted.

"Then tell me how you keep a relationship going for close to two fucking years and then bring a baby into it? Tell me that," I roared once more. My anger had hit an all-time high.

"Let's separate them," Officer King said to his partner.

"No, I'm fine. Just get him out of my face," I told them.

Officer King escorted Kevin and took him into the kitchen. I looked at Paulina, who was drowning in her own tears over in the corner. As much as I hated to admit it, her present state tugged at my heartstrings. I had to go over and say something to her. I even embraced her when I got within arm's distance.

"Don't cry, Paulina," I said.

As soon as those words came out of my mouth, she opened up a floodgate of tears.

"I'm so sorry." She bawled as she embraced me back.

"It's okay," I tried assuring her.

"They said that if I didn't tell 'em what's going on, I could get charged for withholding evidence from them. Then they started talking about how much time these offenses carried. And I got scared," she explained.

"It's okay, Paulina. It's okay," I assured her, hoping that my words would soothe her mind.

"Think the kidnappers are going to find out the cops are now involved?" Paulina asked me.

"I sure hope not."

"Well, do you really believe that Kevin's mistress called them?"

"Yes, I do."

"You think she knows this address?" Paulina's questions continued.

"I'm gonna find out," I assured her. Then I laid my head against hers. This was a bonding thing that we did. It was a sign that we were putting both of our heads together.

It took the SVU detectives another twenty minutes before they arrived. One was a female cop and the other male. Both were Caucasian and they had to be in their late thirties or early forties. When they entered my home, the female cop introduced herself as Detective Kelly, and the male introduced himself as Detective Mann. Immediately they started giving Kevin, me, and Paulina the third degree.

First they wanted to know where the ransom letter was. So I grabbed it from the kitchen, but before either of them would take it, they slipped on a pair of plastic gloves. After they read it over thoroughly, they asked if we had verbal communication with them yet? Our answer was no. Next they wanted me to recall when I first noticed that my children were missing. So I went through the spiel again. Then they looked to Kevin and wanted to know when he left town, and had he made any phone calls to anyone before he left? Then they wanted to know what kind of business he was in? And did he owe anyone money? I listened intently to the answer, and he insisted that he didn't. After that, they wanted to know if any of us had enemies? Everyone answered no. In my former life I had a slew of enemies when I was stealing cars. The car owners wanted my head on a stick, while other car thieves envied me and wanted me locked up or dead. But that was over ten years ago. My hands are clean now.

After the questions died down, they wanted to take a look at the kids' rooms. I escorted them to Little Kevin's bedroom first, and Kevin followed.

"Has anyone come in here since the children were kidnapped?" Detective Kelly asked.

"Yes, I've come in here a few times," I acknowledged.

"Yeah, I've come in here several times, too," Kevin confessed.

"Did you touch anything?" Detective Kelly wanted to know.

Kevin answered first. "No, I didn't."

"I touched the blankets and sheets. I also opened the closet doors when I first started searching for them," I admitted.

"Did you notice anything missing or out of place?" Detective Mann chimed in.

Kevin and I both searched the room with our eyes and then we both answered, one after the other.

"No," I said.

"Yeah, I don't see anything out of place or gone," Kevin agreed.

"Okay, well, we're gonna seal this room off until we can get a forensic team to come in and take fingerprints," Detective Kelly announced.

"Okay," I said, and then we all exited the room.

We entered Kammy's bedroom next and both detectives asked us the same questions, and our answers were pretty much the same. On our way out of Kammy's bedroom, Detective Kelly asked the question I believe she was itching to ask from the time she came through the door.

"Did either of you have anything to do with the kidnapping of your children?" she boldly asked.

By this time we were all walking back down the staircase, so I stopped in midstep and looked back at the female detective. "Of course not! What do you think we are? Monsters?" I snarled at her.

"I'm sorry, but that's a question we have to ask," she insisted.

I continued down the steps, while Kevin reassured them that we wouldn't dare have our own children kidnapped or even put them in harm's way, for that matter. They didn't comment one way or another, but they managed to write down everything we said.

We settled back down in the living room and the forensic team showed up about ten minutes later. They immediately went into action by dusting and fingerprinting every window, front and back door, sliding glass patio door and the children's bedroom doors. The coming and going in and out of my house, like a revolving door, was irritating the crap out of me. I had mentioned before that I didn't want to cause a scene or bring any attention to my residence, but it seemed as though that concept had gone right out the window. It's like no one cared.

I confronted the detectives. "Hey, can you get your police buddies to stop running in and out of my house, please? See, Kevin, this is exactly why I didn't want to get them involved. They're gonna fuck around and be the reason why we don't get our kids back," I complained out loud so that everyone in the house could hear me.

"Can you please make them stay in the house?" Kevin inquired politely, getting the detectives to cooperate with us.

Detective Mann looked at his partner and nodded his approval. Seconds later, she walked over to the forensic team and instructed them to try to keep disruptions to a minimum and make themselves a little more discreet.

"We're going to have one of our technicians come in and put a recording and GPS device on your home phone so we can monitor every call that comes in here," Detective Mann stated.

"I couldn't care less what you guys do at this point," I replied nonchalantly. I really wanted them to just leave me alone. But I noticed quickly that wasn't going to happen when Detective Kelly walked back over to where I was and sat down next to me.

"Let me ask you a question," she started off.

"I'm listening," I said.

"Are you and your husband planning to pay the ransom?"

"Yes, we are," Kevin blurted out from a few feet away.

I looked over at him and gave him the meanest expression I could muster up, because in my mind I'm saying to myself, *She wasn't talking to you,* and then I'm wondering, *How in the hell are you gonna come up with the rest of the money?* Not to mention, he's the reason why we're in this shit, to begin with. If his black ass had been here and not laid up with that other bitch, playing house, our children would be here, safe and sound.

To add insult to injury, I know she's the reason why the cops are here. I know she's the one who called them. I have no doubt in my mind, and one way or another, I'm going to find out.

Detective Kelly kept her attention on Kevin. "Do you have all the money now?"

"No, but we're getting it," he told her.

"Why do you ask?" I wanted to know.

"Because we want to be of assistance when the trade is made," she revealed.

"Oh no, we don't need y'all help with that. We can handle it on our own," I protested.

"But I'm afraid that's the way it has to be," she stated.

"What do you mean?" Kevin blurted out.

"It means that the moment we got the call and walked through that front door, we're now involved," she explained.

"Hey, Kelly, let me speak with you for a second," Detective Mann inserted.

Detective Kelly stood up from the sofa and followed her partner to the other side of the room. They spoke for a few minutes and on a few occasions looked at me. After going back and forth for a couple of minutes, they both returned to where I was sitting. I waited patiently to hear what they had to tell me. From the look on her face, I knew right off the bat that I wasn't going to like what she was about to tell me.

"I just got word that we're going to have to hand this case over to the FBI," she informed me.

A sense of dread and panic ripped through my whole soul. Hearing that the FBI was taking over my kids' kidnapping case rattled my nerves, and my anxiety level spiked up to an all-time high. Seeing how all this was about to unfold, I knew it would have a direct effect on me getting my children back. Not to mention that having the Feds involved might derail my plans of pulling off the two car-heist jobs for Nick. What the hell was I going to do now?

"Is there a way you can handle this and not the Feds?" I wondered aloud.

"No, I'm afraid not. My partner said they're already on their way," she answered.

My questions continued. "So, what happens now?"

"Well, as of right now, I'm going be the team leader, so I will be monitoring everything until I'm relieved by the federal agents."

"And what will the agents do when they get here?" Kevin chimed in.

Detective Kelly started off by saying, "They will sit everyone down in here and do their own interview."

"No way! Are you serious?" I whined. I dreaded the thought of having to answer another round of grueling questions from a different set of law enforcement officers. I knew federal agents were more stringent with their protocols, so I was about to go on a roller-coaster ride.

Meanwhile, the detective was schooling me on what was to come in the foreseeable future, once the federal agents arrived at my home. Something told me to excuse myself so that I could use my cell phone and text Nick without anyone seeing me do so. At first, I battled with the idea of telling him that the cops were now involved, and the Feds were being called in, too. After mulling over the fact that the Feds could start following me, or put a GPS tracker on my car, I felt it was absolutely necessary for him to know what was going on, especially because of the type of job we were about to do. I certainly didn't want to bring any heat to the action. If I didn't tell him, he'd probably think that I was trying to set him up.

"I'm gonna go and lie down for a few until the federal agents get here," I announced, and stood up on my feet.

"You okay?" Paulina asked from across the room.

"Yeah, are you all right?" Kevin asked as well.

"Yes, I'm fine," I told them both, and left the room.

As soon as I walked into my bedroom, I closed the door behind me and locked the door. I headed into the bathroom and closed that door, too, so that I could get a little bit more privacy. With my phone in hand, I started texting Nick's phone and when I got to the part: **Don't call me, I'll call you**, I immediately decided to erase the message and call him instead. He answered on the second ring.

"Yo, what's up?" he greeted.

"There's been a slight change of plans," I whispered.

"Why are you whispering?"

"Because cops are in my house," I continued whispering.

"Why the fuck are the cops there?"

135

"Because someone called and reported my kids' kidnapping."

"Who would've done that?"

"I think Kevin's fucking mistress did it."

"You know that's gonna be a problem, right?" Nick said.

"Yeah, I know, that's why I called you."

"So, what are they saying?"

"They're saying that the Feds are coming in, and when they get here, they're gonna take over the case. So, as soon as we hang up, I won't be able to call you back. I'm just gonna have to come where you are."

"I don't know, Ava, that's kind of risky," Nick said. He seemed doubtful and I feared at any moment he was going to pull the plug on this job. To deter him from doing that, I said, "Listen, Nick, I know what you're about to say, and I know you're not feeling too good about me doing that job, but I can't afford for you to take it away from me. This will be the only way I'm gonna be able to get my kids back. Kevin isn't gonna be able to come up with the rest of the money for the ransom."

Nick remained quiet, as if in deep thought, so I applied more pressure. "Look, I will leave here if you like. I would leave here the first chance I get, and won't return until both jobs are completed."

"And where would you go?"

"I'll come to your house. Stay there," I suggested. This was the only conclusion I could come up with. I figured this would be the only solution that would make him feel secure and confident that the Feds wouldn't derail his mission to get both cars.

"What are you going to tell Kevin?"

"Fuck Kevin! He lost all his privileges in this household after I found out about that bitch in Richmond!"

Nick fell silent for a moment; then he said, "Well, how are you going to get away without being noticed?"

"Don't worry. I'll make it happen," I assured him.

"A'ight, well, if you can get away undetected and make it to my spot without being followed, then I'm with it."

I instantly became filled with excitement. "Yes! Thank you, Nick. I promise I will not fuck this up," I promised him.

"You better not. Now, get out of there as soon as you can."

"I will," I told him. Then we both ended the call.

After the call disconnected, I erased Nick's number from the call log and then I saved his number under the name Domino's Pizza. I knew that I would be spending the next couple of days over at his house, so I began gathering a few things that I could stuff inside of a tote bag without making it look like I was leaving for a few days. Whatever I packed away, it couldn't be bulky. So I thought of the perfect thing, and that meant two pairs of dark spandex and dark-colored shirts. I even grabbed a dark fitted cap from my closet, too. That way my face could be obscured a bit from anyone recognizing me. After I shoved those things into my tote bag, I grabbed two pairs of panties and the bras to match and placed them inside as well. From the looks of things, I was ready to go, but I knew that I had to wait to see the agents first. Because if I left before they got here, it would look bad on my part. It would make me look like a suspect rather than a victim of child kidnapping. So I retired to my bed and watched a little TV until I heard a knock on my bedroom door.

"Who is it?" I asked.

"It's me, Kevin."

"What do you want?"

"The FBI is here. And they wanna see you," he announced.

"Okay, I'll be down in a second," I told him.

Instantly flushed with fear and trepidation, I lay there on my bed and wondered to myself what was about to happen next. Were these people going to give me a hard time, like the Feds did JonBenét Ramsey's parents? They treated those people like monsters and accused them of murdering their daughter after they found her body. Damn, I hope my situation wasn't going to end up like that.

I finally pulled myself together and dragged myself downstairs to meet face-to-face with the FBI agents awaiting my arrival. There were two Caucasian men standing downstairs. They were talking to both detectives and Kevin when I approached them.

Kevin introduced the agents to me. "Ava, this is Special Agent Byrnes and Special Agent Ryan."

"Nice to meet you, ma'am," the shorter one named Byrnes said while shaking my hand.

Then I turned and shook the taller gentleman's hand. After I released Agent Ryan's hand, he started off with his spiel about how things were going to go from this moment forward, so I stood there and listened.

"So Detective Kelly has informed us that they've interviewed you guys, but we're also going to do a round of questioning. We don't have to bring in a forensic team because they already have one here. However, we will conduct a neighborhood investigation. I'm sure you already know that many kidnapped victims fall prey to someone who resides, or who has visited someone, within the neighborhood. There's even a possibility that someone within the neighborhood has witnessed the incident, but will not realize the importance of what they saw until they've been questioned by law enforcement, or made aware of a missing child through the media. Nine times out of ten, someone has seen or heard something," he started off saying.

"Is that even necessary? I mean, I know you're trying to do your job and all, but I wanna keep this as quiet as possible," I stated.

"Don't you want to find your children?" Agent Ryan asked. He sounded sarcastic.

"Of course, I do, but the kidnappers left strict instructions for me *not* to call you guys, or else I won't see my babies anymore," I stressed to him.

"Kidnappers leave that particular demand in the ransom letters as a scare tactic, and because they don't want to deal with law enforcement. They know that once we're in the picture, there's a high percentage that we're going to find out who they are; and when that happens, we're going to prosecute them to the fullest extent of the law. So don't worry about that," he insisted.

"What about the ransom itself? Should we pay it?" Kevin wanted to know.

"Do you guys have it?"

"I'm working on it as we speak," Kevin replied.

But in my mind I knew he didn't have it and he was blowing smoke up their asses.

"From what the detectives say, the deadline is less than forty-eight hours from now?" Agent Byrnes asked.

"Yes, they said they're gonna contact us in seventy-two hours and that's when we should have all of the money," I interjected.

"How much do you guys have on hand now?" Agent Byrnes wanted to know.

I looked over at Kevin, since I didn't have the answer to that question.

"I have most of it," Kevin told everyone standing around, but he was lying.

I don't know why he wouldn't just tell them the truth.

"Do you think you're going to be able to come up with the rest by the deadline?" Agent Ryan asked.

"Yes, I'm working on a few things. So, yes, I will have it," he lied once more.

Boy, did I want to burst his bubble. Expose him for the fraud that he was and tell them everything about the bastard. Instead, I bit my tongue and stayed levelheaded so that we could come to an agreement on something that would bring my children back to me, safe and sound.

"So, after you talk to the neighbors, what's gonna happen?" I pressed them.

"Well, a part of the process of talking to the neighbors is to get a sense of who they are. Identify if they're registered and known sex offenders or not. We'll search out every guest that any of your neighbors have had in the recent weeks, whether they visited frequently or had an extended stay. We'll even collect information to determine if they have a relevant criminal history. That includes running license plates," Agent Ryan explained.

"What about the Ring cams? Every one of my neighbors have 'em," I suggested.

"Oh, don't worry, if they're operable, we will get the footage," Agent Ryan chimed back in.

"Damn! Why didn't I think of that?" Kevin blurted out.

I just gave him an evil stare. He got a glimpse of my stare and closed his mouth.

"Do you mind if we set up and install a trap and trace on your cell phone and home telephone?" the same agent asked.

"No, I don't," I answered back, even though I knew it wouldn't be wise being as I was communicating with Nick through my cellphone. But how could I say no?

"Good, because this would allow us to tape-record and document all incoming calls. It's important that we monitor all communication coming in and going out," Agent Ryan added.

"Are we going to have to stay confined to this house?" I spoke up.

"Why? Is there somewhere you have to be?" Agent Byrnes asked.

"No, but I was planning to make a run to the store," I told him.

"In my experience it's best that the parents of missing children stay close to the home just in case we need them to speak to the kidnappers," Agent Byrnes pointed out.

"Kevin is here. He can do it," I suggested.

Both agents and the detectives looked at Kevin for clarity. He gave them a head nod.

"Okay, well, I guess you can be the point of contact," Agent Ryan told Kevin.

"What does that mean exactly?" I wanted to know.

"It means that all decision-making will go through him, and when the kidnappers finally make contact, he would be the point of contact," Agent Ryan explained more.

I immediately started to protest, because I didn't want Kevin making decisions for my children. He lost that privilege not being here when they were kidnapped. But when I realized that I would be slipping out of the house the first chance I got, and not returning until I had the money in hand for the kidnappers, I decided against it.

"Would you guys, at any point, be willing to take a polygraph test?" Agent Byrnes asked Kevin and me.

I instantly became offended by the question. "What do you mean, would I be willing to take a polygraph test? It sounds like you're starting to treat me like I'm a suspect," I challenged.

Agent Byrnes chuckled. "No. No. No. It's just standard protocol, Mrs. Frost. We ask everyone in the household who's a victim of kidnapping and abduction," he further explained.

"Well, I don't have a problem with it," Kevin assured him.

I gave him a long stare, trying to get over the insinuation that I had something to do with my kids being kidnapped, but then after a few seconds, I let out a long sigh and agreed to having one done if necessary.

"Great!" Agent Ryan said. Then he clapped his hands together and stated that they were going to create a command center in the kitchen and start working on the neighbors' interviews.

I took a seat on the sofa and watched as the federal agents took over and the local detectives took a backseat. After a couple of hours of the agents delegating work assignments to the local authorities, the handful of individuals dispersed after their shift was over. I even watched as Kevin walked away from the hustle and bustle of things to take a phone call. It wouldn't surprise me if the call was from his mistress. Fucking bitch! There was no doubt in my mind that she called the cops over here. Because no one else would've done it. My father definitely wouldn't have done it. If he had, he would've warned me first.

So I will have my day with that whore. Just as sure as my name is Ava Frost. I will confront her, and it won't be pretty. I'm going to blow up on her like Armageddon and she's not gonna know what hit her. And it will all be in the name of my children.

CHAPTER 24

Kevin

"**W**HY ARE YOU CALLING ME RIGHT NOW? I TOLD YOU I WOULD call you back?" I whispered to Ty as I made my way into the garage. I looked over my shoulder to make sure that I wasn't being followed.

"I was only calling to check on you. See if you guys heard anything from the kidnappers," she said.

"Ty, did you call the cops and made a report that my children were kidnapped?"

"No, I didn't. Why would you ask me that?" she wanted to know.

"Because the fucking cops just showed up at my door claiming they received an anonymous call, and you were the only person who knew about what was going on," I lied. Ava's dad knew about the kidnapping, too, but I needed to put her in the hot seat to see if she'd crack.

"Okay, okay, I'll admit that I called them," she blurted out. "But I only did it because I felt like you guys needed help getting those kids back," she admitted.

"Ty, you really did it this time," I snapped at her.

"I was only thinking about the best interest of the children," she tried to explain.

"But I didn't need you to do that, Ty. You don't think we have our own kids' best interest at heart? You don't think that we know what we're doing?" I raised my voice unexpectedly. When I realized what I had done, I looked over my shoulder to see if anyone had come into the garage. When I saw that no one had, I let out a long sigh. "You crossed the line, Ty," I continued in a lower tone of voice.

Ty apologized at once. "I'm sorry, Kevin. I didn't mean to get you this upset."

"It's not about getting me upset. It's about meddling in business that doesn't concern you. Now the FBI is crawling all over my place. Ava is upset about it, and now the kidnappers are bound to find out about it. You really screwed this up," I let her know.

"Baby, I'm so sorry. How can I make this up to you?" she pleaded.

"You can't, Ty! You can't come back from this. And what's so crazy about all of this, Ava called it. She told me that you did this, and I didn't believe her. Like, I literally took up for you and told her that you wouldn't dare do anything like this. I would've bet money on it. But I was wrong. You were all over it. And because of it, we might lose our kids."

"Baby, don't say that. You gotta think positive. Besides, you said the Feds are involved, right? They're pros in that area, so they're gonna make sure they get your kids back. Watch!" she boasted.

"Yeah, you better hope and pray they do," I replied, gritting my teeth; then without giving her notice, I ended the call.

After I shoved my cell phone back down in my pocket, I headed back into the house. As soon as I entered the room where Ava was, she stared me down. It felt like she could see right through me. It was apparent that she knew I had been talking to Ty. Yeah, she was a pro at reading me. And right now, guilt was written all over me. I tried to avoid her by walking in the direction of the kitchen, but she got up from the sofa and followed me. I watched her through my peripheral vision as she stormed in my direction.

Of course, I reached the kitchen before she did. However, as soon as she crossed the entryway, she walked up behind me and let me have it.

"You were talking to your bitch, huh?" she hissed over my shoulder and into my ear.

I turned around and faced her. "I was talking to a business associate of mine. I was trying to see if I could get the money for our kids' ransom," I lied.

"Bullshit! Let me see your phone," Ava instructed as she held out her hand.

Refusing to give her my cell phone, I knew I had no other choice but to come clean with her. Besides, what's the worst that could happen? She already knew about Ty and the baby. I figured if I started being transparent with her from this day forward, then maybe I could turn this thing with us around because a divorce would tear my children up inside. I've also heard that it was cheaper to keep her.

"Okay, you're right. I was talking to Ty. And you're right, she did call the cops and reported the kidnapping," I finally said with a solemn face.

"I fucking knew it! I knew the bitch called them," Ava said, only loud enough so that I could hear her. It looked like she was biting her tongue.

"Calm down! Please don't make a scene," I begged her quietly.

"Does she know the problems she caused by running her fucking mouth?" Ava said as she gnashed her teeth together. "I swear, if she becomes the reason why I lose my kids . . ." she started to say, but then she fell silent.

"I know . . . I know . . ." I agreed with Ava, hoping this would help keep her calm.

"See what happens when you bring outsiders into our family? She's a fucking thorn in our side, Kevin, and you let her in because you couldn't keep your dick in your pants," she gritted at me.

"And I take full responsibility for it."

"You taking full responsibility for this shit show you created doesn't make me feel any better. What would make me feel better is putting a gun up to her head and pulling the fucking trigger." She chuckled. "Yeah, that would make me feel really good."

"Please don't get all worked up," I pleaded with her.

"What do you mean, don't get worked up? I'm already there. Look around you," she urged me as she pointed to the FBI agents walking around freely in our home. "It's just a matter of time before the kidnappers find out they're here, and then what do you think is gonna happen?" she asked me, her eyes starting to become glassy.

"Let's stay positive and remember that at the end of the day, they want the money. That's their main objective. Once we hand that over to them, we'll get our kids back," I said confidently.

"You better be right," she said, punching me in my arm. Then she stormed off in the direction of the refrigerator. I immediately grabbed my arm and massaged where she hit me. I watched her as she grabbed a container of leftovers from the top shelf and headed over to the microwave to warm it up. It was some food that she'd cooked, but I couldn't tell what it was from where I was standing. But I knew whatever she had cooked, it was good, and it would be even tastier the day after, because Ava was a great cook. She could cook anything. I'm talking soul food, Caribbean food, Cuban food—you name it, she could cook it.

"Hey, Mr. Frost," I heard a voice ask me. I turned around to see who was speaking. Ava turned around, too, and we realized that it was Agent Byrnes. "Can I talk to you for a moment?" he asked me.

Ava took her attention completely off the contents in the microwave and turned it toward the agent and me. I followed him back into the living room and I heard Ava's footsteps trailing behind. We walked to an area by the hallway bathroom and stood next to it. I figured he wanted to stop here because he gave us just a little bit of privacy. He opened his hand and revealed an iPhone and began to explain to me that the phone belonged to my neighbors Patsy and Andy, who lived directly across the street from us. He also stated that he was about to show me some video footage that their Ring cam caught at the time my children were abducted. He definitely had my full attention after he announced that. I zoomed in on the phone, while Ava looked over my back.

"Whose phone is that?" Ava asked.

"Your neighbor Patsy Giles, from directly across the street," Agent Byrnes said as he programmed the video to play.

Ava and I looked intently as the video began to roll. The agent held the phone in his hands the entire time. We watched as a dark-colored vehicle slowly drove by our residence. I squinted my eyes to see if I recognized it, but I couldn't. It was too dark outside, and before I could blink my eyes, the car was gone. A few minutes later, a dark-colored van pulled up directly in front of our home and stopped. The size of the van was so big that it obscured the entire view of the front of my house. I couldn't see the front door or the side of my home where the side patio door was. My heart literally sank into the pit of my stomach. I shook my head with disgust and let out a long sigh. "This is useless. The freaking van is black. The tint on the window is black. So we aren't gonna be able to see anything," I complained.

"That's gotta be the bastards who took our babies," Ava commented.

"Yeah, I was thinking the same thing," Agent Byrnes agreed.

I hunched my shoulders and threw my hands in the air. "Unless someone gets out of the passenger side and we can clearly see them, then this is useless," I added.

"Let's wait and see," Ava suggested.

Seconds later, we all saw movement as the van shook a little bit, which indicated that whoever was inside was getting out. Then the movement stopped. We stood there and watched the video for the next five minutes while nothing happened. Not even a car drove by the neighbors' Ring cam.

"This must be when they're in my house," Ava spoke up. "Just thinking about it is giving me the chills," she added.

"Damn, I wish that I had been here," I interjected, punching the bathroom door. This shocked everyone around me. Everyone in the room turned their attention toward me. When they realized that I had only lost my cool for a moment, they turned back around and continued doing what it was that they were doing.

For the next ten minutes, we watched as the time dragged on. There was no motion. Not even a car rode by the neighbor's Ring cam. But then approximately twelve minutes and sixteen seconds later, the van moved. Ava gasped and covered her mouth. "This must be when they put them in the van," she said.

"Yeah, it appears that way," Agent Byrnes agreed.

I shook my head in disbelief as I imagined the culprits taking my children away in that very moment and then driving away from my house seconds later.

After the van vanished from my neighbor's Ring cam, I walked away from Ava and the agent and headed back into the garage so that I could be alone and let off some steam. Ava followed me. The second after she closed the door to the garage, she said, "You know if you would've installed outside cameras like I asked you to, there's a good chance that we would've seen the people responsible for taking our children out of this house."

"Please don't come out here and beat me up," I replied.

"I'm not trying to beat you up. All I'm saying is that—"

Before she could finish, I interrupted her. "I know what you're saying and right now I don't wanna hear it."

"Well, you're gonna hear it!" she roared. Her eyes turned blazing red. At one point it looked like horns were starting to grow out of her skull.

"Look, Ava, I don't wanna fight with you. I know I fucked up, okay? So stop reminding me of it," I told her.

Then I walked away from her and headed outside through the door of the garage so that I could get some fresh air.

I took a walk down my block to clear my head. All kinds of thoughts began to run through my mind. Thoughts of where my kids could be. Were they okay? Were the kidnappers mistreating them? Had they been fed? And I even thought about who could've pulled this off. I could admit that I've done some shady shit in my past, but did I do something so bad that it would make someone come and take my kids away from me? Not only that, who knew where I lived? To my recollection, not too many people. The list was short. So, hopefully, I'd be able to narrow it down and get to the bottom of this.

CHAPTER 25

Ava

IF KEVIN THOUGHT I WAS GOING TO RUN DOWN BEHIND HIM AFTER he stormed outside, he must not know me like he thinks he does. What I was going to do was get my things ready so I could slide out of this house before the agents got used to seeing me around here. My mission was to get to Nick's place without being followed—and that's what I intended to do.

I entered back into the main house from the garage, and both agents leading my kids' kidnapping case were in a huddle talking among themselves. I started to get their attention, but they were engrossed in what they were discussing, so I eased by them and headed upstairs. I figured now would be a good time to get out of the house, especially while they were preoccupied.

I scanned the entire living room for Paulina, but she was nowhere to be seen, so I continued up the staircase to my room. She must've heard me coming upstairs, because she opened her bedroom door just enough to extend her hand out and pull me in. After I entered her bedroom, she closed the door behind me and gave me an alarmed look.

"What's wrong?" I asked.

"I heard the agents saying some very bad things about you," she whispered.

"What did they say?" I whispered back. She made it very clear that she wanted this conversation to only be heard between her and me.

"They think that you set your own kids up to be kidnapped," Paulina said.

Taken aback by Paulina's claims, I immediately developed a lump in my throat and instantly tried to swallow the ball of stress, but it wouldn't go anywhere. So I placed my hand over my neck and tried to swallow again. But the stress wouldn't subside and panic set in my face.

Paulina became on edge. "Are you okay?"

"I need to sit down," I told her as anxiety began to take over my body.

"Come on over to my bed," she insisted, escorting me in that direction. After I took a seat on the edge of it, I took a deep breath and then I exhaled. Meanwhile, Paulina sat on the bed next to me and started rubbing my back in a circular motion.

"Just relax and breathe in and out," she instructed me.

Suddenly the lump in my throat began to dissolve and the anxiety started subsiding. I was beginning to relax just a little. After a few minutes passed, I began to collect my thoughts and a burning sensation of wanting to know more prompted me to probe Paulina for additional answers.

"Did they say why they thought that I would do that?" I wanted to know.

"Well, they talked about the affair Mr. Frost is having and said this would be a good way to get back at him."

"Get back at him how?"

"By having him pay the ransom and you keep it," Paulina elaborated.

"Which agent said that crap?" I asked, gritting my teeth.

I was infuriated by these false accusations. I mean, how dare those morons say those harsh things about me? I love my children. I would never put them in a situation like that, especially over money, not to mention plot against my husband just to get the ransom money. What kind of person would I be? I would never toy around with my kids in that way. Are those freaking agents insane? I mean, do I strike them as that kind of mother? That's coldhearted and evil.

"The shorter one said it and his partner agreed."

"Freaking assholes!" I grumbled.

"Calm down!" Paulina urged me.

But I wasn't really feeling anything she was saying. What I wanted to do was storm out of this room and scream at everyone in here. Accusing me of orchestrating my children's kidnapping to get back at my husband! What a slap in the face that was to me. I mean, here I was on the verge of having a nervous breakdown because someone took my children away from me and these idiots think that I did it.

"Please let's keep this between us," she pleaded with me.

I hesitated for a second and then I said, "Don't worry, I will. But do me a favor."

"What is it?" Paulina asked.

"I'm gonna slide out of here so I can figure out a way to get my babies back. I can't let them see me leave, so I'm gonna need you to do something to distract them."

"What will I do?"

"Fake like you're having a seizure or a heart attack."

Paulina stood there for a moment and then said, "Okay, let's do it."

Excited by Paulina's willingness to help me, and anxious to get out of there, I told her to hold on a minute while I grabbed my tote bag with all my things inside, including my car keys. I returned to her bedroom, less than two minutes later, and instructed her to walk downstairs ahead of me. I followed her closely so that my shoulder tote wouldn't be noticed. As soon as we got to the bottom of the stairs, Paulina stepped to the side so I could slide by her and then she collapsed onto the floor. As soon as she hit the floor, I dropped my tote bag on the floor and kicked it to the side so that none of the agents could see it.

"We need medical attention over here! I think she's having a heart attack," I shouted. I fell on my knees and cradled Paulina into my arms, while she held one hand over her heart.

Special Agent Byrnes and Agent Ryan both ran over to where Paulina and I were. Other officers followed and I was immediately instructed to move out of the way. One of the officers got on the radio and called for paramedics. Before I knew it, I was ushered completely out of the way. As I backed away, I peered through the bodies standing around Paulina, just to get one last look at her, and I must say that she was playing the role of a heart attack victim very well. Everyone's attention was on her, so I figured now was my chance to leave the house. At that moment I grabbed my tote and slid discreetly out of the living room and exited the side door of the house.

My heart started beating a hundred miles per minute and my breathing pattern changed, too, as I made my way out of the house. I must have looked over my shoulder at least ten times before climbing into my car. I even looked around the surrounding area to see if Kevin was anywhere nearby. When I realized that he wasn't, I started the ignition and drove out of the driveway as quietly as I could.

The last thing I wanted to do was bring attention to myself. I waited until I had gotten halfway down the block before I put the pedal to the metal, and when I finally did, I was out of my neighborhood in less than 15.2 seconds. Nick's house was my destination and I had to get there before he got worried that I wouldn't show up. I know him and if he thought for a moment that I wasn't coming to do the job, he would replace me in a heartbeat. I couldn't have that, especially now.

CHAPTER 26

Kevin

I HAD ONLY BEEN AWAY FROM THE HOUSE FOR ABOUT TWENTY MINutes. When I saw the paramedics leaving my driveway, that alarmed me so much that I shot off running in the direction from almost a block away. I was thinking all kinds of crazy things. Was it Ava? Paulina? My brain was thinking of all kinds of scenarios. But I knew that I wouldn't get a clear answer until I got into the house.

When I reached my home, I burst through the front door, and I was greeted by Agent Ryan. "Where were you? We were looking for you," he asked me.

"I was taking a walk. Who just left in the ambulance?" I didn't hesitate to ask.

"It was your housekeeper. She had a heart attack," he explained.

"Wait, is she all right?"

"I can't say right now. What I can say is that she's in good hands."

"Where is my wife? I didn't see her car outside."

"We don't know. We were looking for her, too. My paramedics

had some questions they needed answered and she just disappeared."

"So you didn't see her leave?" I asked him. I needed clarity. I mean, there was a lot of law enforcement in my home and he's telling me that no one saw Ava when she left. That's strange.

"No, I'm afraid not," Agent Ryan replied.

"Well, can you say about how long she's been gone?"

"I'm guessing about ten to fifteen minutes."

"Well, does she even know what happened to Paulina?"

"She was here when your housekeeper collapsed at the bottom of the staircase. She screamed for help, and immediately after we told her to move out of the way, she got up and disappeared on us."

"And you're saying that no one saw her leave the house?" I asked Agent Ryan.

"Nope. We tried to call her, and her phone went straight to voicemail. We tried to call you, too, but your phone kept giving us a busy signal, like it was out of service."

"I don't know why," I said, pulling my cell phone out of my pocket and flashing it in front of him. "It's working perfectly fine."

"Well, could you call your wife and see if you can get her on the phone?"

"Yeah, sure," I said. I immediately dialed Ava's number, and when the call connected, it went straight to her voicemail. "It's going to her voicemail, but I'm going to try it again," I told him as I pressed the REDIAL button. But once again I got her voicemail. After trying to get Ava on the phone for the second time, I ended the call and shoved the phone back into my pocket.

"Where do you think she went to?" Agent Ryan asked.

As badly as I wanted to tell him, *Nick's place,* I couldn't get up the nerve to do so. I knew that I would bring intense heat on Nick if I sent the Feds over to his place to look for Ava. He wouldn't understand it. So I played the clueless role and acted like I had no idea.

"Who knows?" I finally said. Then I walked away from him.

I headed to the bedroom I shared with Ava to see if anything was out of place. When I looked in the dresser drawers, I didn't see anything amiss. Then I walked into the closet, sifted around the clothes she had hanging up, and I didn't see anything missing there, either. But as I turned to head back out of the closet, I noticed that her Louis Vuitton tote bag was missing. She only used the tote as an overnight bag, so it instantly hit me that she wasn't coming back tonight. From where I was sitting, it didn't take a rocket scientist to know she was heading over to Nick's place. One part of me wanted to call Nick and rip his ass apart. I wanted to tell him that I knew what was going on, but then I realized I couldn't do that. Not while the Feds were here. Nick wouldn't ever forgive me if the Feds got wind of who he was and what kind of activity he was into. So I was gonna have to swallow this hard pill and wait until Ava showed back up.

I knew I had to get my mind off Ava being over at Nick's place. I decided to call Ty. I walked into the bathroom, closed the door, and locked it behind me. I turned on the bathroom shower so that the agents wouldn't hear my conversation.

"Another callback so soon?" Ty commented after she answered on the second ring.

"I just called to tell you that while I was walking back to my house, I saw an ambulance leaving my home," I whispered.

"Why are you whispering?"

"Because I don't want the federal agents to hear me talking."

"Where are you?"

"In my bathroom."

"So, why were the paramedics there?"

"They said that my housekeeper had a heart attack, so they took her to the hospital."

"Oh, my God! Will she be all right?"

I let out a long sigh. "I pray she will be," I said.

"So, where is Ava?" Ty asked.

"I don't know. The agents said that she left right before the paramedics got here."

"Well, that's strange," Ty remarked.

"Tell me about it," I agreed.

"So, wait, are you telling me that she knew your housekeeper had a heart attack?"

"Yes."

Ty hesitated for a moment and then said, "Now, that *really* is strange."

"The federal agents thought so, too."

"So, where do you think she could've gone?"

"Not sure," I lied.

I absolutely knew where Ava was, but I couldn't risk being heard—whether over a taped conversation or from the other side of the door.

"So, are you going to the hospital to check on your house-keeper?"

"Of course, I am. But I've gotta wait until she's admitted first. I'm gonna give her about two hours to get settled in and then I'm going to go up there."

"Any news about your kids?"

"No, not yet," I answered.

"Well, keep me posted."

"I will."

"Love you."

"Love you more."

CHAPTER 27

Ava

I<small>T DIDN'T TAKE ME LONG TO GET TO</small> N<small>ICK'S GARAGE.</small> A <small>NORMAL</small> twenty-minute drive took me thirty because I decided to take the longer route. Making sure that I wasn't being followed to Nick's place was a priority. I couldn't afford to have the Feds follow me there and find out that he was operating out of a chop shop, and he was heavily involved in car boosting. Nick would kill me, and I know that I would never see my kids again, especially without his help. This job was important to me, and if I wasn't able to carry it out, I'd definitely lose my kids forever.

When I walked into the garage, Nick was in the middle of a conversation with one of the mechanics as he peered under the hood of a classic 1965 Chevy Impala. Both sides of this huge garage were filled with new and classic cars, all with price tags of at least $100,000. This garage had about two million dollars' worth of inventory under its roof, if not more. It was definitely a cash machine.

As I walked farther into the garage, Nick finally got a glimpse of me through his peripheral vision, and he turned around. His eyes lit up instantly and then he began to walk in my direction with open arms.

"So you made it?" he said.

I smiled back. "Barely," I commented.

"No one followed you here, right?" He wanted to be sure.

I sighed heavily. "Noooooo! I got a clean getaway, trust me," I assured him.

"Well, good. You know that I can't afford to have the heat showing up here. I'm sitting on an empire, and if they found this place out, they'd ruin me."

"I know, I know," I acknowledged.

"Good, now let's go into my office and talk about this gold mine we're about to discover," he suggested, leading the way.

I followed Nick into his office and placed my purse and tote bag on the chair next to his desk. "Is that all you brought with you?" he asked.

"Why, was I supposed to bring more?"

"Come on, Ava, you know we're supposed to be together," he expressed as he stood before me. I could see that he was wearing his heart on his sleeve. It was very apparent that he was not ready to move on. I mean, for God's sake, it had been over ten years and he's still talking about us being together. I swear, I was not up for this conversation. I was only here to get these jobs done so that I could get the money I needed to get my kids back. That was it.

"Nick, let's not do this now, please," I begged him. I was not in the proper head space to talk about him and me. I only wanted to focus on paying my kids' ransom and having them returned to me. Other than that, I really didn't have the mental capacity to take on anything else.

"You know that if we were together, you wouldn't be going through this right now," Nick remarked. "I'm respected around here. No one in their right mind would've walked in a house I owned and kidnapped my kids. That would never happen because I protect mine."

"Well, lucky you." Nick knew I believed this on some level,

too, but I was not up for feeding his ego when my life was upside down and my kids' lives were in peril.

"It doesn't have anything to do with luck. It's about respect—and you know it. Apparently, your husband doesn't have any."

"Okay, Nick, I get it," I replied sarcastically. "We don't have to rehash this all over again. I know where you stand."

Nick threw his hands up in the air. "Look, I'm not trying to beat you up or anything. I'm just stating facts."

"And I said, I get it. Can we talk about something else?"

Nick was willing to change the subject. "Have you heard anything else from the kidnappers?"

"Nope."

"What are the Feds saying?"

"They aren't really saying anything. I mean, they have the phone at home tapped. They've got agents in the field talking to my neighbors, my kids' teachers, and anyone else they can think of to talk to."

"So they don't know anything about me, right?" Nick made it a point to ask.

"Of course not," I responded.

"Do they know about the mistress?"

"They do now."

"Well, they may send an agent up there to talk to her," he said.

"They might."

"Have you ever thought about the possibility that she could be behind this?"

"I thought about it. I mean, she has motive. To get them out of the way so that she could have Kevin all to herself," I said. Then I thought about that statement for a second and it made me sick to my stomach. "But I swear to God, if she did, I'll kill her myself. In fact, if given the chance, I would kill anyone who had something to do with taking my kids away from me."

Nick chuckled loudly and slapped me on the arm. "See, that's the Ava I know and love." Then he turned around and walked behind his desk. He opened the top drawer and pulled out a rolled-up tube of canvas paper and I immediately knew it was some form of sketch. Maybe even a map of some sort. He laid it down on the desk and rolled it out flat. "Come here and let me show you something," he instructed.

I walked over to the desk, leaned over, and realized it was a map of the terminal where the shipping containers were loaded, off-loaded, and stored.

"Didn't I already see this?" I reminded him.

"Not this one. I just found out the vessel that's bringing our second shipment will be docking on the north side of the terminal, instead of the south. I wanted to show you the layout so you can get familiar with where you gotta be, and the distance you'll have to take the car to."

"What would this container look like?"

"Look for a blue container with the word 'Capital' stamped on the side of it in white letters. It will be stored right there, in row ten," Nick said as he pointed to the exact place on the map where the containers would be.

From the looks of the map, the container was the last one in this particular row.

"Okay, I see," I said, zooming in on the layout.

"Got any more questions for me?"

"Not right now. But I'll let you know if I do," I answered him while continuing to study the map.

Nick saw how engrossed I was and left me alone in his office, returning to the garage area.

I let out a long sigh, sat down in the chair behind Nick's desk, and said, "Well, Ava, time to rock and roll!"

CHAPTER 28

Nick

I HAD AVA FOLLOW ME BACK TO MY HOME AFTER WE FINALIZED THE details of tomorrow's heist. During the drive I called ahead and had my house manager straighten my place out.

"Hey, Skip, I'm on my way to the house, so I'm gonna need to make sure everything is in order," I told him.

"What's your ETA?"

"Ten minutes."

"Okay, well, I'm on it," he assured me, and then we ended the call.

I probably looked in the rearview mirror a dozen times at Ava as she followed me, and I couldn't help but wonder what life would've been like if she hadn't left me for that sucker-ass husband of hers. We would be good right now. My house would be hers. Her kids would be mine and things would be perfect.

While thinking about my past relationship with Ava, I received a phone call from Kevin. I started not to answer his call, but then I figured it would be important for me to find out what was happening on his side of town.

"Hey, what's going on?" I asked.

"Nothing much, man," he replied in a low whisper.

I became concerned. "Why are you whispering?"

"I don't want the officers to hear me talking on my phone, so I'm talking low in my bathroom."

"I'm so sorry you're going through this," I told him.

He let out a long sigh. "Yeah, I appreciate it. I'll get through it though."

I got straight to the point. "So, what can I help you with?"

"I just tried to call my wife and she didn't answer. And I know she's with you, so that's why I called."

"No, she's not with me," I replied, knowing that I was technically telling the truth. Ava was not in my car. I was alone.

"Come on, Nick, I know she's with you. I mean, where else could she be? Besides, she took her overnight tote with her, so that let me know that she wasn't coming back tonight."

"Well, again, she's not with me. But if she happens to call me, I'll let her know that you're looking for her."

"Nick, cut the bullshit! I know she's with you, and I know why she's with you, so hand her the phone," Kevin said.

"Kev, she's not with me, man," I said, trying to hold my composure.

I mean, how dare this piece of shit try to disrespect me after all I've done for him. Ungrateful-ass motherfucker!

Kevin huffed loudly. "Look, Nick, don't send her on that run. I'm warning you."

"What? Is that a threat?" my voice boomed. Even though he was whispering, and his tone was low, I could hear the anger and discontent in his voice.

"Take it the way you want. Just don't send her on that run."

Instead of reacting the way that I wanted, I chuckled, because this guy had obviously grown some balls in the past twenty-four hours. Plus, he was dealing with a false sense of reality if he thought that he could threaten me and I'd be all right with it. Once again I'd let him slide, because I knew he was under a lot

of stress—being that his kids were just kidnapped—and now he felt like he was losing his wife, too.

"Hey, look, buddy, I'm gonna go ahead and let you go on that note. But if I hear from your wife, I'll let her know that you're looking for her," I told him. Right before he was about to speak, I disconnected the call on purpose. Immediately after ending the call, I manually blocked him from calling me back.

Upon arrival at my place, I parked in my two-car garage and had Ava park her car inside, alongside mine. The moment she exited her vehicle, I told her about the phone call I had just had with Kevin, and she chuckled loudly and said, "Fuck him! His mistress! And his fucking baby! No one is going to stop me from doing what I have to do to get my kids back. And I mean, *no one*," she spat out defiantly.

It was apparent that she was disgusted by him, his indiscretions, and she wasn't going to let anything stand in her way of making this run for me. This gave me hope that after all was said and done, she might consider getting back with me.

Immediately after we entered the house, I grabbed her things and put them in the guest room. En route back to the kitchen, I heard voices. As I entered the room, I walked into Ava grilling my house manager.

"So, what exactly do you do?" Ava asked.

"I take care of things around the house," he answered casually.

"So you're a housekeeper?" Ava wanted to know.

Skip smiled nervously as he glanced over at me. When he turned his attention back toward Ava, he said, "Nope."

"So, then, what do you do?" Ava's questions continued as she took a seat on the bar stool placed in front of my kitchen island.

"He makes sure things are running smoothly around here," I chimed in.

Ava looked at me suspiciously. "Yeah, right," she said. "I know why he's here."

"Oh, really?" Skip chuckled nervously again.

"Do tell," I encouraged her. I was very curious to hear what she had to say.

"You got him here as your watchdog to make sure no one tries to come in here and rob you for all that money you've got stashed in this house," she divulged.

I looked at Skip and he looked at me. As soon as I turned my attention back to her, I smiled and said, "You're absolutely right."

"I knew I was," she responded confidently.

"Well, now that the secret is out, and my shift is over, I guess I can leave now," Skip announced.

"Okay, but before you leave, do one more walk around just to make sure every part of the house is locked and secured."

"Gotcha!" Skip said. As he was exiting the kitchen, he said his goodbyes.

After Skip disappeared around the corner, Ava mentioned she was hungry.

"Whatcha got in here to eat?" she asked.

"Anything you want," I bragged.

"Well, cook me something."

"Whatcha want?"

"Surprise me."

"Say no more," I said, heading to the refrigerator.

I knew right off the bat what I was going to cook for her. She loved a great chicken Oscar, with grilled asparagus, and that was exactly what she was going to get tonight.

"Want a glass of wine while I whip this meal up?" I asked as I grabbed some of the ingredients from the refrigerator.

"Absolutely," she said.

"Well, help yourself to anything you find in the wine cooler behind you," I insisted, pointing to the dishwasher-sized glass refrigerator that was built into the lower cabinet space next to the kitchen sink.

While she retrieved a bottle from the wine fridge, I grabbed two wineglasses from the cabinet on my side of the kitchen and placed them on the island.

"Why don't you do the honors," she suggested, and handed me the bottle.

"Don't mind if I do," I replied eagerly. After I popped open the bottle, I poured her a half glass and then I poured my own.

"Let's make a toast," I proposed as I held up my glass.

"To what?" Ava asked as she held her glass up next to mine.

"Let's toast to us, making moves, and getting your kids back."

Ava smiled. "Cheers!" she said as we pinged our glasses together.

Immediately after we both took a sip, she added, "Hmmm . . . this is good!"

"Yeah, it is," I agreed as I watched her swallow what she had in her mouth and then take in another mouthful.

"Hmmm . . . this is going to get me ripped," she commented playfully.

Instead of responding, I smiled because I knew what she said was true. And if so, hopefully, I could have my way with her. Fingers crossed!

CHAPTER 29

Ava

AFTER THE DELICIOUS MEAL AND A BRIEF REST, IT SEEMED LIKE time flew by quickly. Before I knew it, it was time to go on the heist. I hopped in the car with Nick, and he took me back up to his garage, where I met the driver Hank, whom I was going to ride shotgun with tonight. After we were introduced, I hopped in his truck and we rolled in silence for the entire thirty-three miles that it took to get to the Portsmouth terminal, where the British Marque Rolls-Royce was awaiting my arrival in the shipping container. As Hank drove up to the gate of the terminal, he showed his ID badge, his pickup manifest, and then we were allowed through the gate.

"You ready?" he asked as he pressed his foot down on the accelerator, making the engine roar as it moved forward.

"Ready as I'll ever be," I commented. My heart was beating like crazy. It had been years since I'd last stolen a car, especially one of this magnitude. I was about to steal a Rolls-Royce with a price tag of $28,000,000. The Boat Tail Coachbuild Edition. There were only two built in the world. And I was about to put my hands on one of them—if I managed to pull this job off.

"I'm gonna drop you off near the operating machine to my left, but I won't be stopping the truck fully," he informed me.

"I'm gonna have to jump out while it's still moving?" I asked nervously.

"Calm down. I'm gonna slow it down to about ten miles per hour," Hank clarified for me.

I let out a loud sigh. "Okay. I think I can manage that," I told him. Then I took a deep breath and watched him as he decreased the speed of the truck. The part of the terminal we were driving down was partially lit. Containers were stacked everywhere, as tall as ten to fifteen containers in the air. The cargo ships were only a few feet away, parked at the ports with containers stacked high on them as well. Also in view were dozens of forklifts, reach stackers, swap bodies, ISO tanks, and quay cranes, which were operated by pier workers. The height of these things was enormous, towering at least 450 feet, with booms long enough to reach across the width of an entire ship.

The sight of them was unbelievable. Actually, the contents of these containers were even more unbelievable. Like, for instance, some of these containers were probably listed on the bill of lading for one thing, while something entirely different was inside of them. Not to mention, the longshoremen who had been working on this terminal robbed these containers on a daily basis. So I needed a piece of the pie.

Hank broke my train of thought. "You ready?"

I looked ahead and saw that we were within feet of my drop-off point. "Let's get it," I confirmed.

"All right, when I count to three, open the door, step down on the ladder, slide around the door, close it, and then jump down to the ground. Got it?"

"Got it. But will you be picking me up from the same spot?"

"Yes, I will. Now the shipping container's on your left. You got twenty minutes to get that car, get into that other container, and make it back here," Hank let me know.

"Nick didn't tell me that," I complained.

"Well, I'm telling you."

"But I'm gonna need more time than that."

"Twenty minutes is all you get. Because that's how long it's gonna take me to circle around this pier. Now go!" he shouted.

I jumped at Hank's sudden outburst, but quickly regained focus on my cue to exit the truck. As instructed, I climbed out of Hank's truck, firmly planted my feet down on the foot ladder, and then I slid to the side just enough so that I could close the door. A couple of seconds later, I hopped down onto the ground with a pair of bolt cutters to access the air lock, the software device to open the car, and the fake key fob to start the ignition.

Strapped with everything I needed, I ran in the direction where the container was stored. This landmark was the south corner of the terminal, and it was called the depot.

"Okay, baby, where are you?" I whispered after pulling out my pocket-sized flashlight.

I began walking and counting the rows of containers that would lead me to the row I was looking for. I was searching for row eleven, with a stack level of seven containers on top. After walking around in what seemed like a maze, I finally found what I was looking for. I could hear angels singing in my mind. I immediately grabbed the bolt cutters from the messenger bag strapped over my chest, stuck my mini flashlight in my mouth, then pointed it directly at the lock so that I could snap it loose.

"Here goes nothing," I mumbled with the flashlight firmly positioned in my mouth as I placed the sharp mouth of the blades around the lock and held tight to the handles of the grips. With all the strength I could muster, I squeezed the handles and watched the blades snap the lock apart. *Pop!*

"Yes," I said with excitement after seeing the lock dangle from the latch connected to the door.

Without hesitation I snatched the lock off and stuck it in my messenger bag, right along with the bolt cutters. Then I opened the doors to the container. As the doors sprang open, an imaginary light came down from heaven and shined on this $28,000,000 automobile. I couldn't believe that I was actually looking at this thing. It was right here in my face. "Okay, snap out of it, Ava. You gotta get in this car, and get it out of here," I said aloud.

Going with my first thought, I entered the container and pulled out the software device that Nick supplied me with. I pointed it at the car door and keyed in the four-digit code. Within seconds the vehicle chirped and the car door unlocked. I quickly opened the door and climbed into the car. After I sat firmly in the seat, I reached back into my messenger bag and grabbed the fake key fob Nick had given me.

"Here goes nothing," I said, sticking the key into the ignition.

And what do you know? It started it up that instant. I revved the ignition quietly, not to draw attention, and then I let my foot off the accelerator. I then applied my foot to the brake, put the car in drive, and then eased my foot back off the brake, and put my foot to the accelerator. I slowly backed the car out of the container, making sure I had enough room to maneuver without scraping the side doors of the car.

With precision I backed the car out of the container, and then I stopped it, giving me just enough room between the back of the car and the container so that I could close it. Once I got out of the car and closed the doors to the container, I climbed back in, put the car back in drive, turned left, and drove around three stacks of containers. This direction took me to the closed-off and nonactive side of the terminal. This section was designated for broken and abandoned containers. No one frequented this area, for reasons of safety and labor, so this was the best route to get this car to its destination.

I cruised at a speed of twenty-five miles per hour, carefully driving with the headlights on, between rows of abandoned containers, until I got to my destination. As I was about to make a turn to head toward the container, I was instructed to stash the car. I saw headlights coming my way.

"Shit," I muttered, feeling panicked.

I instantly noticed that a security driver was coming in my direction. I quickly made a sharp right turn to avoid him seeing me. After I realized that he did see me, and had begun to drive in my direction, I panicked even more. I knew that I had to act fast. So I put my foot on the gas pedal and sped off. The Rolls-Royce accelerated quickly. I noticed that the security driver accelerated his vehicle as well and even began to pursue me. To make matters worse, he turned on his siren and it started blaring loudly and his headlights flashed rapidly.

Panting heavily, I tried to lose him by weaving in and out of the containers, but the driver was good, and he stuck to me like glue. My heart was pounding frantically inside of my chest, but that didn't deter me at all. I knew I needed to drive this car with precision and use my skills to dodge the security driver's car.

Finally, after two full minutes of dodging the security guy, I saw an empty container on the opposite side of the terminal, which was the container Nick instructed me to put the car inside. I drove toward the container, pressed down hard on the brake, and then I brought the car to a complete stop, just in front of it. I had to measure the distance of each side of the container with my eyes to make sure the car was in the right position to go inside without getting scratched. Everything looked good from where I was sitting, so I took a deep breath, stepped on the gas pedal, and drove the car straight into the container.

Once the car was completely inside, I shut down the ignition and sat there quietly. Despite everything going on around the terminal, I could still hear the security driver coming. I just had no idea how close he was. I had hoped that I'd lost him on the last two turns. Unfortunately, I wouldn't know that until I got out of the car and walked back out of the container and saw for myself.

After looking down at my watch, I realized that I only had five minutes to get to my pickup point. If I missed the rendezvous, I would be left on the terminal without a way to get off and would risk being seen. With my heart racing at an all-time high, I got up the nerve and slid out of the car and closed the door quietly. Then I moved toward the open doors of the container with swiftness and peered outside. Surprisingly, the security driver was nowhere in sight, so I let out a long sigh of relief.

"Ava, it's time to go," I uttered softly; then I stepped out of the container, closed both doors behind me, and attached the new lock Nick had given me.

Once I saw that the container was secured, I immediately took off on foot and headed in the direction I had to meet Hank. My heart was not only beating uncontrollably, it felt like it was in the pit of my stomach, but I pressed on, sprinting to the pickup destination, constantly looking over my shoulder to make sure I wasn't being followed. After about a quarter of a mile running, I finally saw light at the end of the tunnel when I laid my eyes on Hank's truck. It was waiting in the exact place he told me it would be, so I sped forward.

As I got closer, I noticed that something was off and readjusted my eyes. After blinking a few times, I noticed that it was a little congested at the exit gate. The trucks were parked behind one another, waiting their turn to exit the terminal. There was one problem: The harbor police and US Customs were checking everyone's load before they were allowed to drive away.

I stopped in my tracks, trying to figure out what to do next. Hank's truck was parked on the side, near the exit gate, but he had to pass by the cops before he would be able to leave. I didn't know what to do, so I stood there and thought for a second, panting my little heart out, trying to catch my breath.

"Oh, my God! What if they're looking for the car I just lifted?" I wondered aloud. Unfortunately, I didn't have the answer to my question, and I figured the only way I'd get it was if I headed over to where Hank was and found out what he knew. Then as I was about to take the first step in that direction, it dawned on me that the harbor police could be looking for me. The thought of that being a possibility made all of my insides ache. Anxiety crept into my stomach and planted itself in the pit of it. I wanted to run in the opposite direction, but I knew that I wouldn't be able to get off the terminal if I did. The only way out of here was either through that exit gate or onto one of those container ships—and I wasn't about to get on one of those. Leaving the country wasn't a trip I was trying to make right now, and especially without my children. I needed to build up some courage and move my ass in the direction of Hank's truck before he decided to leave me.

I stood there for a couple of seconds more, giving myself a pep talk. When I got up the gumption to walk toward Hank's truck, I did.

"Just stay calm, Ava. You can do it," I told myself aloud.

It took me about two full minutes to get to the back of Hank's trailer. As I approached the passenger-side door, I saw his face looking forward from the side-view mirror and he looked worried. I knocked on the side of the trailer, signaling to him that I was approaching his rig from the side. He turned his face toward the passenger-side mirror and gave me a head nod, indicating that he saw me coming. When I reached the steps to the passenger-side door, I climbed on them and pulled open the door latch.

"Hurry up and get in here," he instructed as he sat, patiently waiting for me, in the driver's seat.

I climbed into the truck and closed the door behind me.

"What's going on?" I asked.

"They're looking for illegals coming off the ships."

Shocked by his answer, I said, "No way!"

"Yes way. Illegal immigrants are being brought into this place every day," Hank advised me.

"Shit, and I thought they were looking for the car I just lifted."

Hank chuckled. "Oh no, they're looking for human bodies."

"Think they're gonna find some?"

"They might."

"How long you think it's gonna take to get out of here?"

Hank took a quick assessment of what was going on in front of us and said, "Looks like we're gonna be here for at least another fifteen to thirty minutes."

"Think we ought to call Nick and tell him what's going on?"

"You can," Hank replied nonchalantly.

Since Hank didn't seem to feel any urgency to call Nick, I decided to follow his lead. I didn't place the call.

"Well, let's head on out of here," Hank insisted as he shifted the gears of his truck into drive mode. The truck moved forward slowly and got into the line of trucks before him.

While we waited for Customs to inspect his trailer, we made small talk. "So, how long have you known Nick?" he asked me.

"Over fifteen years. What about you?"

"I've only been working for him for a little over two years," Hank revealed.

"How you liking it?"

"It pays the bills. What were you doing before this?" Hank asked.

"I was a stay-at-home mom."

Surprised by my response, Hank said, "No way!"

I cracked a smile. "Yes, I have two little ones that I take care of."

I could tell Hank was intrigued and he wanted clarity. "So this is your first time doing a job like this?"

"Oh no, I used to do this type of work, that's why Nick called me."

"Oh, really?" Hank seemed even more intrigued, so I continued.

"Nick and I used to be a couple some time ago. I used to run his organization before he went to prison," I boasted.

174

"Oh, shit, you're the girl everybody around the shop says is the master of the car game," Hank mentioned.

I nodded my head in a bold fashion.

"Oh, man, you're like a legend!" he continued with excitement.

I chuckled. "Oh no, don't give me that much credit," I refuted his statement.

Before Hank could utter another word, his attention was shifted by the hand motion of the US Customs agent and port security officer motioning him to move his truck forward. He moved the gearshift and the truck started moving forward.

"Here goes nothing," he said.

I watched as the truck pulled up slowly alongside the officers. When Hank moved up to the designated spot, he was told to stop.

"Good evening, sir. Can I see your CDL, travel log, and bill of lading?" the Black port security officer asked, while a white male US Customs agent stood a few feet back from him. Another white US Customs agent stood along the passenger side of the truck, watching things from where he stood. I smiled at him and then I turned forward and played it cool.

After Hank handed the US Customs agent the documents, he attempted to start a conversation with the guy, but he was cut off in midsentence. "So, what's—"

"Just hold tight and we will be right back," the US Customs agent said.

Hank looked at me and I returned the same look at him.

"Well, damn!" I commented sarcastically.

Hank waved the US Customs agent off and let him proceed with what he was doing so that he could get out of there, since they seemed to be done with him. After both men on Hank's side briefly looked at the details of the documents, they took off and walked to the back of the truck. A few minutes later, the port security officer returned to the driver's-side door and requested Hank get out of the truck.

"We need you to open the back," he told Hank.

Hank climbed out of the truck and walked side by side with the port security officer until he reached the back of the rig. I looked to my right and the other US Customs agent was still standing there, watching me like a hawk. He didn't move one muscle.

From where I was sitting, I couldn't see what was going on, but I heard when the doors of the container Hank was hauling opened up. The doors were only opened for a brief time, because a few minutes later, I heard the door close, and then from the driver's-side mirror, I saw Hank walking back around the truck with paperwork in his hands. Before Hank could get back in the truck, four bodies emerged from underneath it and each of them ran in different directions.

"Hey, we've got illegal aliens!" I heard one of the men shout.

I looked to my right and saw the US Customs agent take off running behind one of the people. Even though it was dark outside, I noticed that the people who had taken off into the dark were all men. I couldn't tell you what they looked like, but seeing them take off running from Hank's truck startled the hell out of me. And to see both US Customs officers and the one port security officer take off running behind them threw me for a loop. It was like watching something out of an action movie.

"Did you see that shit? Those motherfuckers tried to hide underneath my rig so they could get off this terminal," Hank pointed out to me after he climbed back into the truck. His face was bewildered and I could tell that he was in disbelief.

"Hell yeah, I saw it. And did you see the officers take off running behind them?"

"Of course."

"Think they're gonna catch 'em?"

"It's just a matter of time. So, trust me, they're gonna find them, even if they have to lock this place down."

"How long do you think we're gonna have to wait?"

"Not sure. Hopefully, it's not too long," Hank said right before powering the truck off. I knew then that we were going to be there longer than expected. I just hoped that while I was still on this terminal, no one would find out that the car I just lifted had been removed from its original container. If that happened, then I would be fucked for sure.

CHAPTER 30

Nick

"H"EY, HEY, HEY, LOOK WHO'S HERE," I SAID WITH EXCITEMENT as Ava walked back through the garage doors of my mechanic shop. I embraced her after she got within arm's reach of me. Hank walked in, right behind her.

"She pulled it off, boss!" Hank revealed as I bear-hugged her like a rag doll, her arms dangling alongside my body.

I kissed Ava on the forehead and released her from my grip.

"I knew you could do it," I praised her.

"I knew she could, too," Hank acknowledged.

"So, did you guys have any problems?" I asked. "You're here a little later than I'd calculated."

"Oh yeah, US Customs had the exit gate closed off because of some illegal immigrants running around on the terminal," Hank began to explain.

"No way," I replied.

"He's not lying. A couple of them tried to hide underneath Hank's trailer while we were leaving," Ava chimed in.

"How did they find them?"

"Customs was searching every vehicle leaving that place, so when it was time to search my rig, the people climbed from underneath there and ran off. Oh, boy, you should've seen the US Customs guys running down behind them. It was a sight to see." Hank laughed.

I chuckled. "I bet it was."

"So, do you think that car I moved is going to be all right, especially with all that heat flooding the terminal?" Ava wanted to know.

"Oh yeah, our car is fine. It's gonna be picked up in a couple of hours and put on another vessel and shipped out in the morning to the Philippines before anyone notices it. Once it gets there, our money will be wired back to the States and we're gonna be richer than ever before," I assured her.

"I hope so," Ava said.

"Don't worry. We got this in the bag," I reassured her.

"So, how will the next run go?" Hank asked.

"It's gonna pretty much go the same way," I replied.

"What time?"

"Plan on getting here before ten tonight."

"All right, well, I'll see you then," Hank said to me. Then he turned toward Ava and bid his farewell. "See you later," he added.

"Yes, see you then," Ava responded.

After the side door of my shop closed, I looked at Ava and asked her if she was ready to go back to my place. Her response: "Thought you'd never ask."

CHAPTER 31

Ava

IT WAS FRIDAY NIGHT, AND WE WERE NOW AT THE FINAL LAP. ALL I had to do was snatch up the classic 1954 Mercedes-Benz W196, which was valued at $29,600,000, drive it to another container, and then drop it off. Easy-peasy! And then I was out of there.

"All ready to go?" Nick asked me while we were sitting in his shop office.

"Yeah, I'm ready to get this over with," I told him. Anxiety had literally consumed my entire body.

"Well, after this, we'll be home free," he stated.

I guess that was supposed to make me feel better, but believe me, it didn't. The only thing that kept me focused about this job was the fact that after it was completed, I would be able to get my kids back. That was the only thing that kept me going.

"I'm using the same key device, right?" I wanted to know.

"Yes, you are. And remember you're gonna have to find a nearby car to attach the GPS tracker to before you leave the terminal. Hank will have the tools you need in the truck."

"Got it," I said. Then I stood up from the chair I was sitting in. Nick escorted me outside to Hank's truck, where he was waiting patiently for me to climb onboard.

"Remember, you got this," Nick reminded me while kissing my forehead.

I let out a long sigh and then I walked off.

"Take care of my girl, Hank," Nick shouted from where he was standing.

"Don't worry, she's in good hands!" Hank shouted back.

Immediately after I climbed into the truck, Hank smiled at me and said, "You ready?"

I smiled back and replied, "As I'll ever be."

"Well, let's get it." He put the stick shift in gear, rattling the engine, and pressed down on the accelerator, slowly driving out of the gravel-filled yard. He hit the horn as we exited the gate.

I watched through the side-view mirror as the dust and rocks kicked up in the air as we rolled out. It was dark out, so I really couldn't see Nick clearly. I could only see a silhouette of his body. And as we drove farther away, he disappeared completely.

I developed huge knots in my stomach during the drive to the terminal. It seemed like the closer we got, the bigger they grew. At the same time I knew that I had to remain calm and stay focused because my kids' lives depended on this last job. So, as Hank finally pulled onto the terminal, he gave me a small box that could hold a tennis bracelet and said, "You're gonna use the tools in this box to deactivate and remove the GPS from the car, right after you drive it into the new container. But remember, you're gonna have to find a car to install it on before you meet back up with me. Got it?"

"I got it," I told him, and slid the box into my messenger bag.

"Take this, too," he added as he pulled a semiautomatic 9mm Luger pistol from underneath his seat and handed it to me.

I hesitated for a moment. "Why would I need that?" I asked him. I mean, I knew how to use it, but why would I need it now, when I didn't yesterday?

"It's better to be safe than sorry," he replied.

"Well, in that case," I said. Then I took the gun out of his hand, made sure the safety was on, and stuffed it down inside of my messenger bag.

"Okay, so we're on the north side of the terminal. I'm gonna drop you off near that gray building that has those three red shipping containers stacked on top of one another," Hank informed me.

"Is this where you're gonna pick me up?"

"Yes, so it's ten-fifteen now. Be back here at ten forty-five sharp, because I won't be able to stop. You're gonna have to be ready to jump on the stepladder."

"Why?"

"Because this is a no-stopping zone."

"Okay, gotcha," I acknowledged. "All right, well, here goes nothing," I declared as Hank eased up to stop at my drop-off point.

"Be careful," he warned.

"I will," I replied, opening the passenger-side door while the truck was gradually moving. I stepped down on the steps, closed the door behind me, and then I hopped down onto the ground. I looked in both directions as Hank continued on. Then I took off in the direction where the container I had to rip off was stored. As I sprinted by the small gray building, I glanced at the one-thousand-square-foot utility-like structured building and noticed all the windows were lit up with the lighting that came from the inside. I even saw movement inside. I couldn't tell you how many people were inside, but I knew there was someone in there and I kept moving.

It felt like I had to run at least a quarter of a mile to get to my destination. As I approached the location where I was instructed to be, I came face-to-face with a block length of at least ten to twelve different-colored shipping containers stacked one on top of the other. I took out my pocket-sized flashlight, powered it on, and continued down the long line of containers, counting them one by one.

"One, two, three, four, five, six, seven, eight, nine and ten," I counted aloud.

The fact that I was in front of the container that contained the 1954 Mercedes-Benz W196, valued at $29,600,000, had my heart racing. Not to mention, my hands began to sweat profusely. I put the flashlight in my mouth and rubbed both of my hands across my pants.

"All right, Ava, time to work," I coached myself.

After I rubbed my hands dry, I grabbed the bolt cutters from my messenger bag and proceeded toward the container. Without hesitation I grabbed the lock firmly with one hand. As soon as I got within arm's distance of it, I attached the bolt cutters to the lock with my other hand and squeezed the handles as hard as I could. Three seconds later, I heard a *Pop!*

"Fuck yeah," I said with excitement after seeing the lock dangle from the latch connected to the door. "Now let's see what's inside," I whispered.

I snatched the lock off, tucked it away in my messenger bag, along with the bolt cutters, and then I opened the doors to the container. When the doors opened, I saw another imaginary light come down from heaven and shine on this $29,600,000 automobile. I even imagined hearing a choir of angels singing. I swear, I couldn't believe what I was observing. I mean, it felt like I had cracked open another safe and was staring at cash, diamonds, gold, and other treasures. It was unreal.

"Come on, Ava, let's get this baby out of here," I told myself.

So, at that moment, I entered the container and pulled out the software device I used with the other car, pointed it at the car door, and keyed in a different four-digit code. Within seconds the vehicle chirped, the car door unlocked, and I quickly climbed inside. After I settled in the driver's seat, I grabbed the fake key fob from my bag. After I had it in my hand, I held it underneath the steering wheel against the magnetic strip and it started instantly. The whole dashboard lit up like a Christmas tree. I revved the ignition quietly; then I let my foot off the accelerator. I applied my foot to the brake, put the car in reverse, and then I slowly backed the car out of the container. Just like with the prior theft, I had to ensure that I had enough room to maneuver without scraping the car's side doors.

With precision I backed the car straight out of the container just enough so that it wouldn't be exposed if someone drove by and so that I could close the container. Once the doors to the container were closed and locked with the new lock I attached to it, I climbed back in, put the car in drive, and drove in the direction it was supposed to go. I headed west of the terminal to the section where the containers were placed and stored to be loaded onto the vessel heading over to Asia in the Philippines. I cruised at a speed of twenty miles per hour, carefully driving with the headlights beaming between the rows of containers. Before I knew it, I had reached my destination. I cruised down the fifth row and looked for container seven.

"Here it is," I said, my words barely audible.

Anxious to get inside, I backed the car up and turned the wheel around just enough so that I could drive it into the container perfectly. Immediately afterward, I put the car in park, hopped outside of it, and raced over to the container with the flashlight in one hand and the bolt cutters in the other. Without the slightest hesitation I grabbed the lock and snapped it in half. *Pop!*

Instantly a sense of relief came over me. I snatched the lock off and shoved it down in my messenger bag and pulled the doors open. As the doors flung open, an odor of death hit me in the face. *BOOM!*

The smell was so unbearable, I gagged and covered my nose. It was dark, so I pointed the flashlight and aimed it into the container. My heart nearly fell into the pit of my stomach. I was instantly paralyzed by what I saw. I didn't know what to do as I stood there and looked at possibly the four illegal immigrants I had seen running away from Hank's truck the night before.

"Fuck! What am I going to do now? I can't move their bodies. And I can't drive the car over them. Shit! Fuck!" I cursed, trying to figure out what to do next.

I immediately pulled out my phone and called Nick, but he didn't answer. I disconnected the line and tried calling him again. Once again he didn't answer.

"Fuck, Nick! Answer your freaking phone!" I rasped, trying my best not to scream. By now, my face was streaked with worry, and I couldn't think about what to do next. Then fear gripped me around my throat and suddenly I couldn't breathe. "I can't deal with this shit right now," I uttered as panic laced my words as I tried desperately to figure out my next move.

I tried calling Nick's cell phone again, but for the third time, he didn't answer, and this pissed me off.

"Nick, what the fuck are you doing that you can't answer my call?" I grumbled, my heart hammering fast. Then out of the side of my peripheral vision, I saw a set of headlights coming my way. I immediately shot right back into the car. Then I realized that I had touched the latch to open the container. I ran back, wiped fingerprints off with the bottom of my shirt, and slammed the door shut. In a flash I ran back to the car, hopped in, and sped off. As I was driving away, I looked back and noticed that the freaking doors to the shipping container were slowly opening back up. My heart began to churn with an enormous amount of fear as I thought about aborting my mission.

"Fuck! Fuck!" I screeched; my mind now clouded with all sorts of "what's gonna happen now" scenarios.

I looked into the rearview mirror and noticed that the car had stopped. This concerned me, because I knew for a fact it had stopped in front of that opened container, so I knew I had to get out of there really quick. But what was I going to do with this car? It was supposed to be parked in that container, so that it could get hauled off to the Phillipines tomorrow. But now, it seemed as though that might not happen. To make matters even worse, I couldn't get in touch with Nick. So, what now?

After driving around the terminal for about two minutes, I realized that this car was sticking out like a sore thumb. The guys walking around were gawking at the car. Then out of nowhere I saw port security cars and US Customs vehicles speeding by me and heading in the direction of the terminal where I found those dead bodies. I knew then that whoever was the driver behind those headlights that I had seen, and had sped away from, had called the authorities. I had to get the hell out of there.

Feelings of trepidation imploded inside of me, and without giving it much thought, I headed in the direction of the main gate. I couldn't wait around to meet back up with Hank, because that would be too risky. I had to get off this terminal ASAP, before they realized I was the one over by that shipping container and that I had stolen this car from another container. As I sped ahead toward the exit gate, I began thinking about how I was going to explain my way enough that the person would let me off without proper paperwork. Just the thought of them keeping me from leaving this terminal gave me an uneasy feeling. Because there was no way I was going to take the fall for some shit I had no involvement in, or get caught up with a grand larceny charge and lose my freedom over this shit. No way! I was getting out of here and Nick was going to have to find another buyer, because I was taking this car with me.

As I approached the gate, I saw a car before me, and the driver flashed an ID-like badge to the guard and then the gate was lifted. This gave me hope that I'd probably only have to show my driver's license and then I'd be let through, too. Then I realized that I didn't have any identification on me. That was a rule that I lived by for as long as I had been stealing cars. Never ride around with your driver's license, because if you get caught, you're giving up your identity to the cops on a silver platter.

So, as I proceeded toward the gate, I cruised slowly alongside the middle-aged white gentleman dressed in a port security uniform. Without hesitation he asked me for my Norfolk International Terminal badge. I smiled and said, "I'm sorry, but I don't have it."

"What do you mean, you don't have it? You need it to get on the terminal," he stated as he looked at me suspiciously. Then he stepped closer to the car door and added, "Do you work here, because I've never seen you come through this gate before?"

"That's because I just started here a few days ago," I blurted out. I swear, I don't know why I said that. It just came out. Even after I uttered it from my mouth, I didn't believe it.

The security officer looked at me strangely and then he put his eyes on the car. "So you work here, and you drive a car like this?"

Before I could come back with a rebuttal, his radio chirped and then someone on the other end said, "We have code 1051 on the north side of the terminal. Lock down all the access to exit points immediately."

Alarmed by what I'd just heard, I sat there paralyzed for a second until he said, "I'm sorry, but I can't let you leave this terminal. I'm gonna have to lock it down."

As he reached down to his waist to grab his radio, panic struck me again. I realized at that moment that if I didn't get off this terminal, there was no chance I was going to be able to pay my kids' ransom and bring them home, safe and sound, because I was going to be hauled away in handcuffs instead. So I unzipped my messenger bag, grabbed ahold of the 9mm handgun Hank had handed me earlier, pulled it out, and aimed it right at the guard.

"Don't touch that radio," I warned him.

"Hey, lady, put that gun away right now," he demanded.

"I'm not putting shit away. But you're gonna pull that gate up and let me out of here right now," I threatened him.

187

"So you're threatening me, lady?"

"Listen, man, just let me out of here right now," I huffed. He was beginning to drain my patience.

"I'm sorry, but I can't do that," he said.

Then he snatched his radio from his waist belt, and right before he was able to press down on the TALK button, I pulled back on the chamber and fired twice into his stomach. He went limp and his body collapsed on the ground beside the car. I looked in the rearview mirror to make sure no one was around. When I noticed there were no cars coming up behind me, I hopped out of the car, leaned in the security booth, and pushed down on the button that operated the gate with the barrel of my gun. When I saw it opening from my peripheral vision, I turned around, jumped into the car, and sped off, doing one hundred miles per hour.

The car literally went from zero to one hundred miles per hour in .6 seconds. It was insane. I knew then that no one would be able to catch me in this car if there was a massive car chase. I didn't want to cause one, so when I got at least thirty miles from the terminal, I pulled the car over to an abandoned gas station and drove around the vicinity of it to make sure that I would be safe to get out. Once I felt like I'd be okay, I parked the car behind the station itself, where it was pitch dark. Then I got out of the car, crawled underneath it, and I finally removed the entire GPS tracking system from the car with the tool kit Hank had given me. Then I threw it into a nearby dumpster.

"Good riddance!" I mumbled before speeding the car back out of there.

My entire drive to Nick's place, I thought about how I was going to rip him a new asshole. I mean, I had just killed one of the port's security guards. I just hoped that he didn't have on a body camera, because if he did, then I was fucked. I guess I would find out later.

CHAPTER 32

Nick

I WAS ALL SMILES WHEN AVA KNOCKED ON MY FRONT DOOR, BUT when I looked behind her and saw the $29,600,000 Mercedes-Benz parked outside, in my front yard, I barked at her that instant. "What the fuck is that car doing here?" my voice boomed.

She pushed me backward into the house and closed the door behind me. "I tried to call you numerous times and you didn't even answer. Now, why is that?" she questioned.

"I didn't hear my phone ring," I lied. I got every last one of her calls. But my number one rule has been while people are in the middle of doing jobs for me, I don't answer their phone calls. I only talked to them *after* the job was completed. I did this to prevent getting set up by the cops if they've gotten arrested during the commission of my job.

"That's bullshit, Nick, and you know it!" she roared. Her eyes were fire red.

"Look, you've gotta get that car out of here now," I warned her.

"And take it where? The fucking police are probably looking for it."

"Did you take the GPS off it?"

"Yes, I did."

"So, why isn't it on the terminal? What happened?"

"The fucking container that it was supposed to be shipped in was already filled up with dead bodies."

"*What?*"

"You heard me. Dead bodies. When I opened the container, there were four dead men inside, and it looked like the guys that I saw last night running away from Hank's truck. And if that is, in fact, true, I believe those fucking US Customs agents did it and hid their bodies in that container, not knowing it was going to be used by us," she explained.

I combed my entire face with my right hand. "How did you get off the terminal?" I wanted to know.

"I shot the guy at the gate after he refused to let me through."

"What the fuck is wrong with you? Did anyone see you?"

"No."

"So there weren't any more cars leaving when you were?"

"There was one car before me. But they had already gone on before I did what I did."

Disgusted by what had transpired, I looked at Ava and said, "You know you fucked this whole deal up, right?"

"Don't blame that shit on me. It wasn't my fucking fault that dead men were in the container that the car was supposed to go in. I tried to call you so you could give me further instructions, but you refused to answer your damn phone," she said, mad as hell.

"Why didn't you find another empty container?"

"Because that option wasn't discussed before I agreed to do the job."

"Well, common sense should've told you—"

Ava cut me off by saying, "Fuck you, Nick! How dare you talk to me like that!"

"But do you realize that you fucked up a twenty-million-dollar deal?"

"Look, just get over it. It's done. Move on and find another buyer."

I instantly shot her a demonic look. "So that's how you're carrying it?" I asked her, spitting venom out of my mouth.

She threw her hands up and waved me off, as if dismissing me. "Nick, I don't have time for this. Just give me my money so I can get my kids back."

"I can't move until that car outside is sold," I told her.

"Are you crazy? I'm not waiting on that. You're gonna give me what you owe me now. And while you're getting my money, I'm gonna make this call to the motherfuckers who have my kids," she insisted. Ava immediately pulled her cell phone and a piece of paper from her messenger bag.

I stood there and watched her as she dialed a number that was written on a piece of paper she held in her hand. After she keyed in all the numbers, she waited for the line to start ringing.

Buzzzzzzzzzz! Buzzzzzzzzzz!

A sudden vibrating sound coming from my sofa caught both of our attention and we looked in that direction. Surprised that the burner phone had fallen out of my pocket when I got up from the sofa to answer the front door, I stood there dumbfounded. I swear, I didn't know what to do or say. But it was clear that Ava was trying to make sense of why I had the phone of the kidnappers. She pulled the phone from her ear with a puzzled expression on her face.

"Look, I know you're wondering why I have the kidnappers' phone," I said.

She nodded and said, "Yeah."

"Well, before you start looking at me sideways, I just wanna let you know that Little Kevin and Kammy have been taken good care of since they were taken from your house," I stated, looking at Ava, hoping she'd have some compassion and understanding.

"So you've had my babies *this whole time!*" she shouted; her voice escalated with each word.

"Wait, hold on," I tried to explain as I took another step.

"No, don't come near me!" she shouted.

"Okay, I won't come near you, but I'm gonna need you to calm down before someone hears you."

"Nah, fuck that, Nick! How do you expect me to calm down when I'm now finding out that the nigga I used to mess with had something to do with the kidnapping of my kids? Now explain that to me."

"I'm trying to, but I'm gonna need you to lower your voice," I said with poise, trying not to ruffle her feathers any more than I already had. I knew I needed to de-escalate this situation before she became a problem for me.

"Look, just tell me where my children are."

"Would you let me say what I have to say first, before I tell you that?"

She took a deep breath, exhaled, and said, "You got two minutes to talk."

"Okay, listen," I said. Then I paused, because I didn't want to say the wrong thing, and after a second or two of mulling over my thoughts, I continued by saying, "This whole thing was just a ploy to get you to do this job for me."

"What! You used my kids as pawns? What kind of sick game are you playing?" she shouted.

"Wait, I'm not done. See, I don't know if you are aware that Kevin owes me a lot of money," I blurted out.

"What the fuck does that got to do with me and my kids?" she screeched.

I could tell that she was getting pretty annoyed now. She was shaking with rage at this point.

"Look, I've invested over two million dollars in Kevin's business, and I have yet to get any of it back. I can't tell you if he's making bad investments, or tricking it up with that new bitch and the baby he's got, but I wasn't feeling it. Every month he had one excuse after the next and I never got a dime back. So I figured that the only way I could get my money back was to take away your kids for a couple of days and put a ransom on their heads," I admitted.

"So, because Kevin owed you all of that fucking money, you made me and my kids suffer because of it?" she hissed.

"Ava, nothing was going to happen to your kids. They are in good hands. I mean, your daughter cried when she woke up and found out she was in a stranger's house, but she calmed down after that. They both ate well. They watched movies. Cartoons. Played games. You name it, they were good," I explained.

But she wasn't feeling anything I was saying. "Nick, where are my kids?" Ava asked again.

"They're here in my house."

"Where?" she pressed.

"Downstairs in my basement."

Without another word Ava turned around and bolted toward the door near the kitchen that led to the basement. Before she could get within three feet of the basement door, I shot off behind her, grabbed her shirt, and yanked her back. She stumbled a bit, almost losing her balance. After she was able to plant both of her feet firmly back on the floor, she grabbed my hand and snatched it away from her shirt.

"Get the fuck off of me! You piece of shit!" she barked. I could see her anger was starting to well up like a volcano. Without warning she hurled a hunk of her spit out of her mouth and onto my face. I instantly saw red as I wiped the spit from my face and examined it in my hand. It was disgusting and I lost it.

From that point it all seemed like everything went in slow motion. I raised a closed fist and lunged right at her, and it hit her smack-dab in the right side of her head. The impact took her out instantly and she hit the floor hard. *Boom!*

CHAPTER 33

Ava

I CAN'T TELL YOU HOW LONG I HAD BEEN KNOCKED OUT AFTER NICK hit me. What I can say is that my head was ringing. My insides felt like they had been knocked out of place and I was dazed. I rubbed my head intensely as I tried to gather my thoughts. When I saw Nick sitting in a chair, watching me from a couple of feet away, fear consumed me like never before. Before I could utter one word, he stormed toward me and stood over me.

"You fucking bitch!" I heard him say while I was trying to stop my head from spinning. "Spitting on me? Are you fucking crazy? After all that I've done for you! That's how you repay me?" he grunted.

"You took my kids from me," I mustered up the will to say as I fought through the pain in my head.

"Yeah, bitch, you fucked my best friend while I was locked up, and then you married that nigga on top of that. Do you know how that made me feel? A bitch that I took off the streets and gave a good life to because her father put her out of the house—and that's the thanks I get? You go off and fuck my best friend?"

"Nick, that was over ten years ago," I tried to reason with him.

"Bitch, I don't care if it was twenty years ago, you don't think I still feel that shit? I gotta see you walk your ass around here, all married and shit, playing mommy to that nigga's kids, when they should've been mine. How fucked-up did you think I feel? You giving my pussy away to that weak-ass nigga? He couldn't even afford to take care of you, that's why I am funding his lifestyle and his businesses. Even then, he couldn't manage his affairs, so I had to step in and do what I had to do to get my money back. See, you got guts. Your husband doesn't. That's why, when I took the kids, I knew you would be the one who would pull the strings to get them back. So, when I found out those two cars were coming in, and how much I could make off them, I knew that no one else would be able to pull that job off, but you. I mean, it's unfortunate that I had to involve you and your kids in your husband's business affairs, so I can get my money back. But that's just how life goes. Just feel lucky that I didn't tie their asses up, starve them, or sell them to some human traffickers. Because you know that I could've gotten a pretty penny from a few guys I know in the business," he commented, and snickered.

At that moment, I became enraged. Just the thought of this bastard selling my kids to sex traffickers had my blood boiling and sent me into a fit of rage. I lifted my left leg, aiming at his groin area, and flung a kick at him. To my surprise, I missed it by an inch and my foot landed in his thigh. This made him furious.

"You fucking bitch!" Nick roared. He reached down and grabbed a fistful of my hair and wrapped it around his hand. He lifted my head off the floor, and then he forced it back down with brute strength. The back of my head crashed to the floor with so much force, I thought my brain would shoot out through my forehead. I knew now what people meant when they got hit and said they literally saw stars. My head hit with so

195

much force, flashes of light invaded my eyesight for at least thirty seconds. I was dazed and confused, and the pain was like nothing I'd ever felt before.

"Nick, please stop! You're hurting me!" I cried out, trying to pry his fingers from my hair, but he wasn't relenting.

"Shut up, bitch! You're gonna take this ass kicking tonight. I'm gonna make you suffer for all the nights I had to lay in bed and think about you fucking my best friend and then have kids by that loser!" he growled. Then he dug his fingers into my scalp, clutching my hair at the roots, filling his palm up with it. Next he began dragging me across the floor. Suddenly an excruciating pain shot through my scalp and radiated over my entire head. I swear, I had never felt pain like it in my whole life. It felt like my entire scalp was being ripped off. I started kicking and screaming.

"Nick, let me go. Let my fucking hair go!" I yelled as hard as I could.

"You heard my mommy! Let her go," I heard a voice shout from the other side of the room. Nick and I both looked in that direction and saw my son pointing a gun directly at us. At that very moment I realized that the gun I was carrying in my waist had fallen out onto the floor. And now my son had it in his hand. Nick didn't know this, but my son knew how to use and fire a gun properly. I had been teaching him how to hold and fire a gun since he was six years old. Right now, he was looking very much like my savior.

"Hey, you better stop waving that gun around before you hurt somebody," Nick warned him as he stood straight up and started walking toward him.

"Leave him alone, Nick," I shouted as I began to pull myself up off the floor.

"He better put that gun away before I take it from him," Nick warned me as he continued toward Little Kevin.

I couldn't get up fast enough to get to Nick before he grabbed ahold of my son. The adrenaline pumping inside of me became overwhelming as I scrambled in the direction of Nick and my son. My only thoughts were to get to my son before Nick did, but it seemed like I was moving in slow motion. Before I knew it, I saw Nick towering over my son as Little Kevin stood there with the gun pointed directly at him. Without a moment's notice Nick lunged toward my son and then I heard the gun go off twice.

Pop! Pop!

Instantly I flinched, shutting my eyes for a second as my heart collapsed into the pit of my stomach. Then a loud thud to the floor followed. I was extremely afraid to open my eyes, but I knew I had to. When I did, I saw my son's body buried underneath Nick's body. I screamed instantly, seeing my son lying there as I saw blood pouring onto the floor. I couldn't believe I was here, and I couldn't help him. I scurried over to grab him because I needed him in my arms, even if it was for the last time. A floodgate of tears began to escape my eyes as I began to roll Nick's body over.

"Momma," I heard a little voice say after my son's eyes opened.

My heart fluttered and my eyes lit up as soon as I heard my baby speak. "Baby, I thought you were . . ." Then I cut myself off in midsentence and grabbed him into my arms.

Little Kev looked down at Nick's lifeless body and asked, "Mama, did I kill him?"

"It was an accident, baby. It was only an accident," I told him. Because there was no way I was going to tell him that he murdered that man. I couldn't allow him to have that on his conscience. It was either tell him it was an accident or make him think he was the hero. Either way I wasn't gonna allow my son to ever think that he was a monster like Nick.

"Where is your sister?" I changed the subject.

197

"She's downstairs in the basement."

I scrambled back onto my feet, grabbed Little Kevin by the hand, and we went down into the basement to get his sister.

"Mommy," my baby called as soon as she laid eyes on me.

I rushed toward her and scooped her up in my arms in milliseconds. She was so happy to see me. While I was holding her in my arms, Little Kevin was hugging me around my waist. I could tell he didn't want to let me go.

"Mommy, are you taking us home?" my son asked.

"Of course, I am," I replied while massaging his head with my free hand.

"Where is that man?" Kammy wanted to know.

"He's dead," Little Kevin blurted out.

Shocked by Little Kevin's outburst, Kammy said, "He is?"

I popped Little Kevin on his head. "Hush up. No, he's not," I refuted his statement.

"But he is," Little Kevin corrected me.

I grabbed his head and tilted it back just so he could look into my eyes. "No, he isn't," I reminded him.

I guess he got the point and didn't say another word. "Now let's get out of here," I told him and his sister.

I held my daughter in my arms and instructed her to hide her face in my chest as we exited the house. I also instructed Little Kevin to keep his eyes closed and I would guide him every step of the way. They both took my instructions very well and we were out of the house in less than ten seconds flat.

"Strap you and your sister in your seat belts," I instructed my son.

While he was doing just that, I started up the engine, looked back at Nick's house, and then I got the hell out of there before any of his guys showed up.

Ava

Off into the Sunset

WHEN I RETURNED HOME WITH THE KIDS, OF COURSE THE FBI was still swarming the place. They had all sorts of questions for me. They even tried to question my children, but I told them that they were off limits for now because of what they've been through. I gave them some bogus story about how I met the kidnappers at an abandoned house about twenty miles away from the location they told me to leave the money. I also highlighted that I didn't get to see anyone's face, nor the vehicle they were driving. But for some reason, they didn't believe me, and I didn't care.

On another note, Paulina was excited to see the kids run through the front door. She grabbed them and held them really tight. I relished their heartwarming moment for a few seconds, but when I realized I had some unfinished business, I instructed Paulina to watch them for an hour or so until I got back. She promised me that she wouldn't let them out of her sight. Knowing this, I grabbed a duffel bag from my hall closet and ran back out of the house. I got into my car and raced back over to Nick's house. Since I left the Mercedes-Benz in full view for the cops to see, I made sure I wiped the car clean of my fingerprints. After I felt like the car was clear of my DNA, I hopped out of it and headed back into Nick's house.

The moment I entered, I emptied out his home safe and grabbed his laptop. Before I left his house, I dragged Nick's body downstairs to the basement and locked it in one of the soundproof rooms. I figured no one would find him for days, maybe even weeks, since you needed a security code to get into the room and I changed it, since I had access to his laptop. I even moved his car into a nearby parking garage. I figured maybe his house manager and people who were close to him would think he left town after the cops came here and found the car I had stolen from the terminal parked out front. I also figured that if the cops' presence was heavy on this property, all of his friends and cohorts would stay clear of it. But we shall see.

It took me several days to pack up my things and my kids. Paulina and I moved out of that Godforsaken house my soon-to-be ex-husband purchased for me and the children. I filed for divorce and put the house up for sale. Kevin didn't fight me about taking the kids to Houston. He knew that I had him by the balls and I would've dragged him into court for the affair, not to mention him having a new baby. He had no idea that Little Kevin murdered Nick, or that I had robbed him for everything he had. He also didn't know that in the next week, over twenty million would be wired to my account. I was set for life. But then, *boom!* An opportunity came through Nick's computer just like that. A 1963 Ferrari 250 GTO, chassis 4153, that was recently sold for $70,000,000 was about to be shipped to the buyer. And guess what? I was about to go and get it, and then that would be another bag. Tell me life isn't good!

If you enjoyed *Amber Alert,* you'll love the continuation of Ava Frost's story. In the next installment, *Hunting Ava,* more lives will be lost, but the life worth saving will be the last person standing. Ava will be reminded that she is a warrior, and she'll have to fight to the death.

CHAPTER 1

Ava

Life in Texas

IT'S BEEN FOUR MONTHS SINCE MY MOVE TO HOUSTON, TEXAS, AND IT has been peaceful. I brought Paulina and the kids with me and we're now living in a beautiful five-bedroom, four-bath, $750,000 home. It also has a three-car garage, and all the amenities to go with it. I could not have asked for a better home. The good thing about it was that I purchased it with cash. I even bought myself a brand-new SUV. In fact, I picked up a $240,000 Bentley Bentayga truck. It came with all the bells and whistles, and I am enjoying it.

My divorce with Kevin is still ongoing, but I will get through it. Since the house is on the market, I heard from the kids that he's living in Richmond with his sidepiece, Ty. I'm sure she loved it when she found out that I filed for divorce. I'm sure she was waiting for that day to happen. He FaceTimes the kids every day like clockwork. He wants to see what's going on and who's around. He knows that Paulina is with me, and that I bought a bigger house. He is also aware that Nick is dead and no longer a threat to us.

Kevin was informed a day later when the cops stopped by our home and questioned us both about the last time we had seen or spoken with Nick. I had Paulina take the children out of the house for ice cream when the cops came by. Kevin told them that the last time he had spoken with Nick was the day after our kids were kidnapped. When it was my turn to speak, I told them that I stopped by his shop to see if I could borrow money for my kids' ransom. When he told me that he couldn't help me, I left, and that was the last time I saw him. I take it that they believed us because they haven't reached back out to us again for further questioning.

After the detectives left, Kevin went into questioning mode to see if I knew anything about Nick's death, but I told him flat out that I didn't. What I did tell him was, Nick had taken me to meet the kidnappers. He handed them the money, got the kids back for me, and then we went our separate ways after that. My story seemed plausible, so I gathered that he believed me. No one knew what really happened but Little Kevin and me, and I made him promise that he wouldn't tell a soul. Not even his father— and he said that he wouldn't.

Thankfully, Kevin wasn't giving me any grief about the kids being in Texas with me. I assumed his mistress and new baby kept him busy to the point where our kids' absence hadn't bothered him so much, and that worked for me.

As usual, he called on a Saturday morning to check on the kids before Paulina took them to their soccer games. I've always tried to stay out of the way, to avoid speaking with him. His pathetic existence really got underneath my skin. Knowing that he cheated and had another family behind my back was the betrayal of a lifetime, and I knew that it was going to take me a while to get over, so I embraced it.

I was in my bedroom when he called my cell phone to Face-Time the kids. Instead of answering it myself, I walked into Kammy's bedroom, where she was, and handed her the phone.

"Hey, Dad," she answered as I walked away and headed back into my bedroom, which was only a few feet away. I could hear the conversation clearly.

"Hey, baby girl, what's going on?" Kevin started off.

"Nothing much, Daddy. Getting ready to go to my soccer game," Kammy replied.

"Are you excited about it?"

"Yes, I am. I think we're gonna win this time, because the girls we are playing aren't really good."

"That's awesome. I wish I could be there to see it," Kevin said.

"So, when are you coming out here to see us?"

"Soon. I just have to take some time off work and then I'll book a flight out there to see you guys," he explained.

"Okay, do you want to talk to Little Kevin now?" she asked. It was apparent that she was more excited about getting ready for her soccer game than talking to her father. Kevin was used to the kids casting him to the side for outside activities, so he didn't take it personally.

"Yes, of course, where is he?" I heard him say.

"He's right here, hold on," Kammy said.

Then I heard her run into the hallway, where Little Kevin was fishing for his kneepads out of the closet.

After she handed the phone to her brother, I heard Little Kevin say, "Hey, Dad."

"Hey, son, what's going on?"

"Nothing much, I just got my kneepads out of the closet and now I'm getting my gym bag, because Paulina is waiting outside in the car to take us to our games," Little Kevin told his father, and then the conversation faded out as he headed into his bedroom.

I didn't time their conversation, but they were on the phone for some time, so I continued doing what I was doing. A short while later, I was abruptly interrupted when Little Kevin walked to my bedroom and handed me my cell phone back.

"Dad wants to talk to you."

Instantly annoyed by the fact that Kevin wanted to speak with me, I took a deep breath and braced myself for what he had to say, while Little Kevin sped off in the opposite direction.

Now facing him via FaceTime, I gave him a nonchalant expression and asked him, what did he need?

Kevin got straight to the point. "Is there something you wanna tell me?"

"What are you talking about?" I was becoming more irritated by the second.

"Tell Little Kevin to come back to the phone," Kevin instructed.

"For what? Just spit it out," I pushed back.

"Was Nick the one who kidnapped my kids?"

Shocked by his question, I swallowed hard on the imaginary lump in my throat and pretended not to have heard his question. To buy myself some time, I asked him to repeat himself.

"You heard me. Was Nick the one who kidnapped my kids?" he asked once again, his eyes laser focused on me.

Since Kevin and I had been together for a long time, he knew when I was lying. I wouldn't give him direct eye contact and the palm of my hands would sweat uncontrollably. Today I had an edge because he couldn't see my hands, so all I had to do was keep direct eye contact with him and he'd believe me.

"Where did you get that from?" I asked, creating another stall tactic.

"Where do you think I got it from? Little Kevin just told me," he stated.

"I don't believe you," I said, looking him straight in the eyes.

"Call Little Kevin right now and tell him to come back in the room!" Kevin demanded.

I could tell that he was getting upset.

"He's not here. He just walked out of the house to go to his game," I lied. I could literally hear Little Kevin downstairs rummaging around in the refrigerator, getting a snack to take with him. Kammy had already walked out of the house to get in the car with Paulina.

"Ava, don't bullshit me! Why would Little Kevin volunteer and tell me that my friend Nick was the one who took him and his sister out of our house?"

"He probably said it because Nick's face was the first one he saw after he paid the guys the ransom money." The lies kept flowing and my story was coming together.

"Stop it, Ava!"

"Stop what?"

"Little Kev told me about y'all's little secret, too."

"What secret?" I pretended not to know.

But deep down in my heart, I knew what Kevin was about to tell me and I instantly got sick to my stomach. I wanted to vomit right then and there, but I realized that Kevin was watching my every move, so I had to keep my composure.

"Since you wanna play fucking dumb, let me tell you about my son's little secret," he started off saying. His eyes doubled in size and spit was spewing from his mouth. "His exact words were, 'Daddy, I wanna tell you about me and Mommy's secret, but you gotta promise that you won't tell anyone else.' So I said, 'Son, I promise I won't tell a soul.' Then he went on to tell me that he heard you and Nick arguing upstairs in Nick's kitchen, because you found out that he was the one who kidnapped him and his sister. Little Kevin also said that Nick started beating on you, so he ran upstairs, grabbed the gun that was on the floor, and shot Nick with it," Kevin added.

Taken aback by this whole conversation, I stood there paralyzed. I was at a loss for words. I mean, how was I going to talk myself out of this one? Little Kevin had just exposed the truth to his father, and now I needed to figure out how I was going to handle things going forward.

"So you don't have anything to say?" Kevin pressed.

"What do you want me to say?" I couldn't lie and say that what Little Kevin revealed wasn't true, because what child at his age would conjure up a story like that?

"First of all, I want to know why you didn't tell me that Nick was the one who kidnapped the kids? And two, don't you think I should've been the first person to know my son was the one who shot and killed Nick? My goodness, I am his fucking father and you're his mother, so you should've been the one to tell me right after the shit happened."

Still not knowing what to say, I stood there, trying to gather my thoughts, and this pissed Kevin off.

"So you're just gonna stand there and say nothing?"

I finally spoke up. "I don't know what to say."

"Why don't you start by telling me the reason why you felt it was okay for you not to say anything about what happened the night you got the kids back? I mean, don't you think that what Little Kevin did is going to affect him later in life?"

"He's gonna be fine," I tried to assure him.

"How can you say that? He fucking shot and killed a man!" Kevin screamed back at me.

"Because after he did it, Little Kevin mentioned that it felt good to protect me," I divulged.

"He's a freaking child, Ava. He's not mature enough to be in tune with his feelings."

"I'm telling you, Kevin, our son is a different breed. He's gonna be fine."

"No, he's not, Ava."

"So, what are you saying?"

"I'm saying that we're gonna have to get him some counseling."

I protested right away. "No way! No one else can find out about this, because if they do, then there's a chance our son could go to jail. I wouldn't be able to live with that."

"If what you said is true, then he wouldn't go to prison, because it would be a case of self-defense," Kevin tried to make me understand.

"No, I can't chance it," I said with finality.

Kevin let out a long sigh. "Look, I'm gonna leave that alone for right now, but we will revisit this later."

"Yeah, whatever," I uttered, my words barely audible. And right when I lifted my free hand to press the END button, Kevin said, "Hey, wait, before you go."

"What is it?" I replied.

"I'm gonna need my part of the ransom back, now that I know Nick was the actual kidnapper."

"What do you mean, *your* part?"

"The part that I gave you. I want that back," Kevin elaborated.

"What makes you think I have it?"

"You think I'm stupid, don't you? I always wondered how you were able to pack up, relocate out of town, and purchase a new house, when I was the only breadwinner in the family? And now it all makes sense."

I let out a nervous laugh.

"You go ahead and laugh, but I know what I'm talking about. Speaking of which, I spoke to Nick's sister, Lacey, right after he was murdered. She told me that all of Nick's money was stolen from his house, along with his computer and some other things. Now that I know that you were the last one there after he was killed, I'm sure you took the ransom money back. So I want my part back and you've got less than a week to send it to me," he warned.

"Do you realize that piece of shit took our kids from us because he figured it would be the only way he was going to get back all the money you owed him?"

"That's bullshit! Don't blame that on me!" Kevin said. It was obvious that he didn't want to take the blame for our children's kidnapping.

"Well, it's the truth. Nick said that you were a fucking loser, Kevin! And that I was stupid for leaving him to be with you. He said that I was better off with him."

Kevin became defensive right away. "He didn't say that."

"Believe what you want, but I'm not sending you a dime. Charge it to the game! You owed it to Nick anyway."

"Listen, you bitch, if you don't send me that money, shit is going to hit the fan."

"And what does that mean?"

"Don't send me my money back and you'll find out," Kevin threatened. "Oh, and before I go, I want you to look at a calendar and figure out when you'll be able to put my kids on a plane and send them back out here to Virginia so I can spend some time with them."

I refuted the idea instantly. "Oh, you can forget that. It will *never* happen."

"And why not?"

"Do you think I'm gonna let you have my kids around that fucking home-wrecker you're laid up with out there? I think not."

"She's not a home-wrecker. And besides, they're gonna have to meet her one day. She and I have a kid together, which is their sibling."

"Do you think I care about that kid being their sibling? It's not happening, so drop the subject."

"I'll drop it for now, but just know that there's no judge in the court system who's gonna prevent me from having my kids around Ty and my daughter," Kevin asserted.

"We'll see about that," I told him right before I abruptly ended the FaceTime call.

After I ended our call, I stood there pissed off at the idea that he wanted me to put the kids on a flight to go visit him in Virginia just so he could parade his fucking side chick and baby around them. Was he crazy? My kids aren't gonna feel comfortable with that dynamic over there. They're just now getting adjusted to the idea that we're going through a divorce. Kevin needs to allow us to get over this first hurdle. Then maybe after that, we can address the fact he fucked around on me and had that baby. But until then, we're gonna follow my lead.

Now fast-forward to the topic about giving him the ransom money back. I could only wonder what he planned to do if I didn't send him his money back. How would he punish me? I couldn't come up with any answers on my own, so I tossed my phone on the bed and slumped down on the edge of it. I figured the only thing to do was wait it out and see what happened next.

CHAPTER 2

Kevin

Back in Virginia

"**T**HINK SHE'S GOING TO SEND YOUR PART OF THE RANSOM BACK?" Ty asked me as she entered the living room, where I was sitting down on the sofa.

"I take it you heard my conversation?" I asked her.

"Yep, I heard every word," she replied, sitting down next to me.

"Can you believe that shit?"

"Which part?"

"All of it. She literally kept that entire night a secret from me. If it wasn't for my son, I would've never known what happened," I said.

"How do you feel about him killing your friend?"

"Well, it's obvious that he really wasn't my friend, especially after finding out he was the one who kidnapped my kids. Besides that, I feel bad for my son, because knowing that you were the cause of someone else's death can be traumatizing, especially for a boy his age. For his mother to have hidden this information has my blood boiling."

"You think she stole money from that guy?" Ty questioned.

"Absolutely. Now that I know that, I want my money back."

"Think she's gonna give it to you?"

"She has no choice."

"What are you gonna do if she doesn't?"

"I haven't figured that out yet, but I'll come up with something," I assured Ty.

Ty leaned in my direction and started massaging my shoulders.

"You look so tense," she commented.

"After just having that conversation with Ava, my body feels more than tense," I told her as she rocked my body back and forth. I tried to relax, but the thoughts in my head wouldn't let me.

"I'm sure the topic itself was a lot to deal with. I can't imagine finding out that our daughter, at your son's age, killed someone, and the other parent kept it from me. No disrespect, but that wasn't the right judgment call on her part. For that alone, she shouldn't have those kids in her custody full-time. I mean, she has clearly demonstrated that she doesn't make the best decisions as a parent. What Little Kevin did is considered a crime, and whether she knows it or not, she's now involved. If the cops were to find out, she would be charged with accessory to murder," Ty expressed.

I sat there for a moment and thought about what Ty had said, and she was right. Ava could get charged for her involvement, and maybe if I reminded her of that, she wouldn't have a choice but to send me my money back. Well, I guess I will find out in time.

Ty spoke up again. "Can I ask you something?"

"Sure," I answered.

"How did you feel when you heard Ava saying that she didn't want the kids around you, me, and the baby?" Ty chuckled as if Ava's comment alone was amusing, and then she said, "Just know that I didn't take it personally, because I know those words came from a place of hurt. To be perfectly honest, I'd probably feel the same way if I were in her shoes."

"So you weren't offended at all?"

"No, I wasn't. I told you, I'd probably feel the same way," Ty clarified.

"Oh, okay, good to know," I acknowledged. Then I dropped the subject about Ava and started talking about our future plans together. "Wanna get married right after my divorce is final?" I asked.

Ty's face lit up. "Of course, baby, I would love that. Oh, my God! Are you proposing to me?" she asked with excitement.

I chuckled. "No! No! No! I'm not proposing just yet. I just wanted to know if we were on the same page about when was a good time to tie the knot."

"Baby, none of that matters. I'm just so excited that you're thinking about making me your wife," Ty remarked.

"How could I not think about it? You gave me a beautiful daughter. Besides, we're like a match from heaven. You complete me, Ty," I expressed to her.

"Awww . . . really? Thank you so much, baby! I really appreciate you saying that," she replied.

Then she leaned in and gave me an intimate kiss on the lips. Sparks started flying everywhere and my manhood stood up.

"Come on, let's go in the room and have some fun before the baby wakes up," I suggested.

Without a word Ty grabbed me by the hand and led me into the bedroom.

It's been about thirty-six hours since I last spoke to Ava. I've tried calling her cell phone and Paulina's, too, and they are refusing to answer. Unfortunately, my children don't have phones of their own, so I'm unable to reach out to them directly. Due to Ava's actions, I see that she doesn't have any plans to return my part of the kids' ransom money. Now I have no other choice but to take matters into my own hands. Things are about to get really ugly, and she will regret this day.

Without further hesitation I picked up my cell phone and got Nick's sister, Lacey, on the phone. She resided in Los Angeles with her husband, Maceo. They had their own chop shop business going on out there. I was sure she'd be interested in finding out who stole her brother Nick's belongings. And just maybe after I brought her up to speed about the latest developments, she might even reward me a finder's fee for the information that I was about to lay on her.

"Hey, Lace, what's going on?" I said.

"Hey, Kevin, nothing much. What's going on with you?" she reciprocated in kind.

"Just calling to check up on you, make sure you're all right."

"Kevin, all I can do is take it one day at a time."

"Are you coming back on this side anytime soon?" I asked.

"Well, I was thinking about coming back that way next week so I can tie up some loose ends with business affairs that Nick started up before his death. Why you ask?"

"Because I need to talk to you about something very serious."

"What's it about?" Lacey asked.

"It's about Nick," I replied.

"What about him?"

"I can't say it over the phone," I told her, using an evasive tone. I was sure after doing that, she knew this was a serious matter.

"I'll tell you what, go get a burner phone and call me back on this number," she instructed.

I agreed to do as she asked. "Okay, give me fifteen minutes."

"All right," she said, and then we ended the call.

Immediately after I shoved my cell phone down into my pants pocket, I grabbed the car keys, left the house, and drove to the nearest corner store to purchase a throwaway phone. With the phone in hand, I sat in my car, powered it on, and activated it. Within minutes the phone was working, so I dialed Lacey's phone number again. She answered on the first ring.

"Hey, what do you have for me?" she didn't hesitate to ask.

"Remember you said you'd pay a finder's fee if someone told you who was responsible for Nick's death and the items stolen from his house?"

"Yeah," she responded, and by her tone of voice, I could tell that I had piqued her interest.

"First of all, what's the finder's fee?" I wanted to know.

Lacey laid it all on the line. "If you're about to tell me who murdered my brother, I'll pay two hundred grand for that. If you could show me where I can find them, then I'll throw in another fifty grand. If that same person has my brother's computer and his money, I will pay a cool million, with no problem."

"So you're saying that if I give you all that information, you'll pay me $1,250,000?" I asked her for the sake of clarity.

"Yes, Kevin, I would. Now tell me who killed my brother," she demanded to know.

I took a deep breath and exhaled, because I knew that after I gave her this information, there was no turning back. I wouldn't be able to recant anything I was about to say.

"Who are they?" she pressed me.

I cleared my throat and said, "It was one person."

Lacey wouldn't let up. "Who?"

"My wife, Ava," I finally said. I swear, after I uttered her name, I could hear a pin drop on the other line. There was complete silence. When Lacey and I began our conversation back up again, I could hear her breathing, but nothing else.

"Ava killed my brother?" she asked. Her voice instantly became menacing. It almost sounded like she was a mechanical robot.

"Yes," I assured her.

"And how do you know this?"

"Because she told me."

"And what exactly did she tell you?"

"She told me that Nick was the one who kidnapped our children. The reason why he kidnapped them was because making me pay a ransom was the only way he was going to get the monies I owed him back," I explained further.

"That's bullshit! My brother had nothing to do with that! He wouldn't have ever done anything like that," she interjected. She really took offense to that accusation.

"No, it's true, Lacey. My son was the one who told me about it first. When he did, Little Kevin told me to promise that I would keep it a secret and not to tell his mom that I knew about it."

"So he's trying to protect her?" Lacey deduced.

"Well, of course, but you know why she told him not to tell me?"

"Yeah, because if you knew she was the one who murdered him, then you would've figured out she was also the one who stole his money and his computer."

"Exactly," I confirmed.

"Have you confronted her about this?"

"Yes, I asked her about it, but she denied it," I lied to Lacey. I couldn't let on that I blackmailed Ava in exchange for getting my part of the ransom back. Lacey would look at me differently and assume that I was okay with what happened to Nick. I wanted to distance myself from that situation at all costs. When you had beef with Nick or his family, there was always hell to pay. Throughout the years I witnessed so many get hurt and even murdered at the hands of these people. They were notorious for making people pay for their bad deeds. Knowing this, I never wanted to put myself in a position to be on the receiving end of their reign of terror.

"Where are you now?" Lacey wanted to know.

"I'm home."

"Is she there with you?"

"No, I live in Richmond now. And she just relocated to Houston."

"Oh, wow! When did that happen?"

"After we got the kids back, she filed for divorce, packed up her and the kids' things, and moved out of the house we shared. After she left, I moved to Richmond."

"Who's at your house now?" Lacey asked.

"No one. We put it on the market. So, hopefully, we'll get to sell it before our divorce is final."

"Do you have her address in Houston?"

"Yes, it's on the divorce filing packet that I just recently received."

"Well, text it to me and I'll handle things from there."

"Wait, hold up, what are you going to do?" I asked. I knew Lacey was ruthless and she'd put a contract out on someone's head without even blinking. I just needed to know what were her plans so I could make sure my kids weren't around when she made her move.

"Come on now, Kevin, you know I can't tell you that."

"I understand that, but my kids are there with her, and I can't let anything happen to them," I made clear.

"Well, allow me to assure you that nothing will happen to your children. They will be perfectly safe," she assured me.

Her assurance didn't do anything for me because I knew my son. If by any chance he was around and he felt like his mother's life was being threatened, Little Kevin was going to do something. I mean, look at what he did to Nick. Now I couldn't disclose that information to Lacey because she was going to want to do something to my son, so I figured the best thing for me to do was fly out there and take my kids out of the house when Lacey sent her goons after Ava. That would be my best bet.

"Hey, listen, I'll tell you what. I'm gonna fly out there and get my kids out of there before the shit hits the fan," I volunteered.

"Be my guest," Lacey commented.

"So, when am I going to be compensated?" I wanted to know.

"Right after we deal with your wife and retrieve my brother's things."

"Can I get an advance?" I dared to ask.

"Are you low on cash?"

"Kinda, sort of."

"Well, text me your banking information and I'll wire thirty grand by tonight," Lacey said.

"All right, thanks."

"Don't mention it. And look, don't alert your wife about what's coming her way, because if you do, we're gonna come after you next," she warned me loud and clear.

"Trust me, I won't."

"Good, now if you hear that she's leaving town anytime soon, let me know."

"Okay," I replied, my mood turned sour at the possibility of me getting hurt.

"Hey, don't sound so down. Look at it this way, since your divorce hasn't been finalized yet. After she's gone, everything that she owns will be yours," Lacey stated, and then she chuckled.

She had a point, but I wasn't in the mood to laugh after she threatened me. When she realized that, she said, "Hey, listen, call me if anything changes, and in the meantime I'm gonna wire you this money, okay?"

"Okay. Thanks."

"Don't mention it," she said, and then we both ended the call.

Immediately after the call ended, I tossed my phone on the passenger seat of my car and sat there in disbelief. I honestly couldn't believe that I just ratted my wife out to Nick's people, and in a couple of hours from now, there would be a hit out on her. And it was all in the name of money. When she was gone, I'd be getting full custody of the kids and the entire payment from the sale of the house. What a win-win situation I was in.

Damn! I just hit the lottery!